Steve's Monkey's Paw

How could Alex resist *this*?

I stood behind her, removing the hair combs, before smoothing her thick, wet tresses. A trickle of rain coursed from her hair down her bare and perfect shade of tan spine into the delightful valley between her very round buttocks. I studied them and handled them, as I unzipped. I heard her tense, small, fearful sigh, which made me want her more, as I took my expanding heavy rod in hand and dragged him across those two superb mounds. She took two halting steps away rom me.

"No, Kara. Stay."

Gran had said, "Strongly willful people can resist," but only as far as *my will AND the paw* would allow. She said I should be "very careful with it" and with what I wanted, because prolonged exposure could weaken a person completely and enslave them to me.

She'd also patted me on the cheek and proudly said she knew I didn't want to do *that* to anyone.

Gran never ever understood the *real* me, and she'd certainly wouldn't get, that *I really wanted this*.

Kara stayed put, as I kicked her robe out my way....

Hesitation *[Published in Playgirl Magazine]*

"I'll get you something of mine to wear, if you don't mind." *(Mind, mind, why would I mind?)* I mutely nodded, as he showed me the bathroom.

I'm not a shower person, but I was so cold, I stripped right away and jumped in. I also forgot the door was cracked open, he'd meant to come right back, but his phone rang. He talked, evidently on a cordless, as his voice moved room to room, while I rinsed off street crud and date makeup—he might as well see the real me, instead of rain smudged me.

I was still a little chilled in the warm shower fog, then realized shutting out the door draft would help, when he bopped in with a robe for me; wearing only a change of boxer briefs.

* * * *

Other Works by Neale Sourna

**North Coast Academies Diary
Steve's Monkey's Paw & MORE
Hobble [An Adult Fiction]**

Steve's Monkey's Paw
(or Steve's Poe Paw) & MORE

Short Stories & Novel Excerpts
Adult Fiction [Explicit]

by Neale Sourna

A ⦿ Fiction
A PIE: Perception Is Everything
Adult Fiction

www.PIE-PerceptionIsEverything.com
www.PIE-Percept.com
www.Neale-Sourna.com

Copyright © 2006 by Neale Sourna

All rights reserved. No part of this book shall be reproduced or transmitted in any form or by any means, electronic, mechanical, magnetic, photographic including scanning, photocopying, recording or by any information storage and retrieval system, without prior written permission of the publisher. No patent liability is assumed with respect to the use of the information contained herein. Although every precaution has been taken in the preparation of this book, the publisher and author assume no responsibility for errors or omissions.

Neither is any liability assumed for damages resulting from the use of the information contained herein.

Duplication or distribution to any other person via email, floppy disk, network, printout, or any other means is a violation of international copyright law and subjects the violator to severe fines and/or imprisonment. This notice overrides the permissions given by any software or hardware used in the production of this work, which are erroneous.

This is a work of fiction. Names, characters, places, incidents, and their juxtapositions are the product of the author's imagination or are used fictitiously. Any resemblance to actual events or locales or persons, living or dead, is entirely coincidental.

Steve's Monkey's Paw Image and Cover © Neale Sourna
Crossed Battleaxes graphic & Aegis graphic © Neale Sourna
HOBBLE Cover concept © Neale Sourna

HOBBLE Photo by the effervescent Sonya Cheren
Makeup by the charming Barbara D'Avilla, both of
Studio f.64, Cleveland OH. 440-888-9317, **www.studiof64.com**
Model *(Author)*: Neale Sourna as "Day"

ISBN **0-9741950-8-1**

February 2006

Published by

PIE: *Perception Is Everything*™   www.PIE-PerceptionIsEverything.com
12600 Rockside RD Box 192   www.PIE.Percept.com
Cleveland OH 44125 USA   www.Neale-Sourna.com

"Doing for the mind, what the body shouldn't."

Published and Printed in the United States of America or the United Kingdom
Not for sale or republication without written permission by
PIE: Perception Is Everything/Neale Sourna

Adult Fiction *[Explicit]*   *www.PIE-Percept.com*   *www.Neale-Sourna.com*
Buy — *HOBBLE* — Now at 1-877-BUY-BOOK, and online internationally

Steve's Monkey's Paw
(aka: Steve's Poe Paw)

[The Complete Short Story]

by Neale Sourna

Whoever came up with "guys don't make passes at girls, who wear glasses" was seriously stupid. Alex's Managing Executive, Kara, wore horn-rimmed eyeglasses, conservatively classy office dress casual, and her dark hair smoothed back in a no frills chignon; all to no avail. She was "definitely, definitely"— *I felt as half-witted and out of my depth, as that idiot "Rainman" around her.*

A wholesome, yet unassuming, sultry brown goddess, who, in my exceedingly learned opinion, was entirely failing to hide her mischievously bouncy breasts and ass under that crisply bland professional façade, which I couldn't believe was deterring Alex. The biggest, most successful and unrelenting sexhound I'd ever known.

It'd been a long while since he'd seen me, so, I'd decided to come out of hiding. I was visiting him at his office and catching up on the last few years and all that kind of thing. He was installing a new piece of phone equipment and software himself.

Not good.

Alex likes to do things himself, that's why he'd opened his own successful business. The man's a true god working with people, female or male, especially female, but he's all left thumbs with anything with cables.

"Um, excuse me, Kara. Alex needs you." She immediately got that look smart women get of "I knew Mr. Know - It - All would need me."

Alex had changed.

When her incredibly fine ass accidentally brushed against

his well-educated crotch, as she entered his personal desk space, he didn't even smirk, let alone attempt to spoon her, as I've often seen him do to those with less obviously well-endowed charms.

The man was not the same.

Kara is *a deliciously big girl* in <u>all</u> *the good ways*, yet he actually backed away, as she leaned on his desk, took the cables of the new hardware and deftly switched the end connections, which we two smart, former frat men hadn't figured out. Why study instructions, which are so often badly and confusingly done these days, anyway. Besides, *Ms.* Know-It-All hadn't looked either.

However, she did look at Alex. A lot. Which he, of course, would never notice, since he *always* gets looked at a lot. The thick, Black Scot-Hispanic hair, the perfect skin, teeth, and musculature, the clear blue eyes, with "all that abundant charm glossing over all that reckless danger," or so states my kid sister, repeatedly.

Lucky Alex.

For myself, women of Kara's quality, *never* look at *me* that way.

I'm "not hideous," as my small-brained sister once gushingly pointed out, but "well, Alex is well *Alex*." Me, I'm just a generic looking Polack, who doesn't turn heads or get the hot cream liquefying and rushing down the insides of welcoming thighs, just because I'm in their proximity.

Silently, we'd both watched her return to her office, which was across from and in full sight of his.

"*She so wants you,* Alex." I got a blank, unfathomable stare from those all too perfect eyes of his.

"What?"

"Kara wants you."

On reading faces.

When you go on cat crawls and bar hops, also know as "pussy prowls" and "bunny hops or skips," with Alex, you become a genius at reading faces. *You, also, hate it. At first.* Later, you get addicted, watching those all too eager faces that are too afraid to approach *the godling* himself, but who ask *me* tips about how best to approach *him*.

Oh, yeah. Put out, then I'll inform you that I may take Alex' leftovers, but he never takes mine.

Reading faces.

Alex had always had very subtle, neutral expressions to hide his true feelings—*pro and con*—for people constantly falling all over him. He'd gotten some newer ones though, since last we'd faced off, making him even harder to read now. But, for a man known for his genial casualness, he was proving with Kara to be unmistakably *too* concise about nearly every movement and tone of voice of his that could be construed as sexual.

Which is odd, since he has utter command of whatever the rest of us will never have; including never having to worry about being taken to task for sexual harassment—except perhaps as a *plaintiff* not a defendant, with the constant offers and innuendo that can gravitate to the man.

And, here he is tipping around on rice paper and eggshells with a bombshell in his sights.

Just look at her. Just *listen* to her, with *that voice,* as smooth as hot cum sliding down chilled crystal. She *had* to be at the extreme top of his "to do" list, but he wasn't acting like it at all.

He most definitely *had* changed.

Reading faces.

Kara's open and expressive face is a true joy to read;

especially, her dark, old soul eyes, which, I absolutely swear *sparkle,* when interacting with Alex. How could he not—?!

"I repeat, again, Mr. Selectively - Hearing - Impaired. The lovely Ms. Kara *wants* you."

"Nice thought, but she's my exec, Steve . . . employee technically, though I'm asking her to go partners because she's brought in so much lucrative business with her innovations." He shook his head, in *my* complete disbelief. "Kara's . . . a friend. *Very* smart, exceptionally capable, absolutely indispensable, a brilliant researcher and innovator. Did I say smart? And—."

"Stunningly beautiful. Seductively gorgeous."

He was silent, while scratching his ear *[a sure little sign of his keeping something to himself]*, then he shrugged, as if all *that* didn't matter.

My god! Was this still Alexander "The Horn," who'd always received comprehensive BJs, handjobs, or fucks in any aperture he preferred to stick it, from practically anyone he ever chose for the blessed opportunity? He really *couldn't* see Kara's obvious but reserved interest? Her seductive . . . everything?

"So, you're *not* dating her?"

"N-no." Nice, but how to get her to notice *me*, beyond basic, common civility because I was in the room, let alone go out with her, was another matter.

A glaring, bright light bulb came on over my head.

Our minds can forget a billion gazillion things, then, at the most crucial, Lucifer-illuminated moment . . . it's there. The number of that cute, dumb girl, who'll do *anything* for little to no coaxing. Or Grandma's monkey's paw. *Damn hideous thing!* Gave me nightmares, as a child. Inherited it with a box of other "memorabilia," better known as old lady crap.

Gran'd sworn someone in the family'd gotten it directly from Poe, who'd written THE story. You know, The Edgar Allen Poe and "The Monkey's Paw".

Oh, yeah, I believed that.

Although, it is amazing how much we don't believe . . . until an intense desire makes it all longingly believable.

Alex and I watched his new tech toy give number, name, time of call, and tons of other profound data; "even from voicemail." He was proud. It was so exciting. Oh, joy. Neato. Yawn. He was completely fascinated by his new plaything. Myself, I watched Kara moving around interacting with the others outside his office, envisioning her strong and well-toned, shapely legs vised around me. And at their center, her dark, humid, triangular arrow of musky lust pointing and directing me . . . .

I'll hit that target, if he won't.

"Hm? What, Alex? 'What am I thinking?' Nothing, really. Let's eat."

Long lunch. Catch up. Here and there pick info about Kara. More catch up. It's been great seeing you, Alex. See yah again, soon. No, I won't be a stranger and wait so long next time.

The usual, insincere bullshit.

Fast car.

Home.

"Where's that damned box of yours, Gran?" Monkey's paw, monkey's paw—.

Ugh! Still goddamned hideous!

I grabbed the brightly furred, bony, blackskinned thing, then put it back; dropped it really, as if it were a flaming, taboo object. I thought hard and long. I needed to be unambiguously correct, and not mess up, like the silly, pathetic, old geezer couple in the story.

Heart pounding, I held that cursed thing and silently wished the precise words of power I felt would work most perfectly. Remember, "in the beginning was The Word."

Of course, typically, it picked then to storm and rage overhead, complete with lighting flashes and tons of rain.

I waited. *And, waited.* Nothing. *Nothing.* For the better part of an hour.

Fuck it.

I went outside to watch bitchy Mother Nature's little I'm God show, and my own vaporizing breath in the chilly, wet suburban night.

One minute later, a sports car pulled up in the wrong direction and jerked to an abrupt, screeching, haphazard stop at my curb, as if it'd been turned off while still geared in drive. Eventually, Kara stumbled out, and hesitatingly walked across the expanse of my yard. No umbrella. *No shoes.* What I'd mistaken for a trenchcoat was a thick bathrobe getting soaked heavily with rain.

Disbelieving my eyes, I breathlessly jumped off the porch to meet her. She came straight to me, and I removed her rainstreaked hornrims.

Her magnificent eyes were scared, confused, and . . . obstinate.

You get ten novena, Gran. Thanks.

"Come inside, Kara."

* * * *

I locked the door, then walked around her. Beautiful, simply stunning—even drenched, pissed, and trembling violently. I reached for her robe; she tried to stop me.

"No, Kara."

She . . . let me, against the hard and futile resolve in her burning, dark eyes.

I opened her robe. *Mother goddamn.* She must've just stepped out of her bath. Completely naked; fresh, clean. *Mine.* I peeled the sopping garment off her, letting it drop heavily at our feet, then walked around again for the full, juicy inspection.

This was all much better than that hormone-induced, mind-crippling notion of her I had had to excuse myself for, when at lunch with Alex . . . to lock myself, like an unrestrained pervert, in a men's room stall, so I could jerk her off my mind.

Which plainly hadn't worked.

I'd imagined Alex oblivious in his office and the others going about their business, while I did *my* business with Kara. Bending her over Alex' big, hard wood desk, with my enthusiastic, swollen cock tightly filling her—back, front, and on her begging knees.

That'd only been . . . a waking wet dream, though. Here was the real, warm deal, in her peerless, naked flesh. My heart beat faster, my nads ached vengefully, as I hardened like pure Carnegie steel for her.

How could Alex resist *this*?

I stood behind her, removing the hair combs, before smoothing her thick, wet tresses. A trickle of rain coursed from her hair down her perfect shade of tan spine into the delightful valley between her round buttocks. I studied them and handled them, as I unzipped. I heard her tense, small, fearful sigh, which made me want her more, as I took my expanding heavy rod in hand and dragged him across those two superb mounds. She took two halting steps away from me.

"No, Kara. Stay."

Gran had said, "Strongly willful people can resist," but only as far as *my will AND the paw* would allow. She said I should be "very careful with it" and with what I wanted, because prolonged exposure could weaken a person completely and enslave them to me.

She'd also patted me on the cheek and proudly said she knew I didn't want to do *that* to anyone.

Gran never ever understood the *real* me, and she'd certainly wouldn't get, that <u>*I really wanted this*</u>.

Kara stayed put, as I kicked the robe out my way, to stoop and caress the underside of her sweet ass with my cock, before resting him along her crevice. Thick, hot, swollen kielbasa on cool, toasty brown buns.

She exhaled another displeased sigh, as I pressed against her, to look down the front of her extraordinary body. I squeezed her breasts, scratching her sensitive chestnut nipples erect and hard as No. 2 eraserheads with my fingertips and nails. My lips and tongue skimmed along the velvety line of her soft cheek and jaw, stopping on the hot, pounding throb in her honeysuckle scented throat.

I listened to her breathing alter with her unwanted, responsive arousal because of *my* touch.

I continued kneading one of her doughy breasts, as I looked farther down her, then gently entangling my fingers in her softly curled, dark bush and grabbed a handful. Snatching snatch. I tugged hard enough for a peek, at the dark, pouting lips between her dimpled thighs.

"Come."

I lead her to my bedroom. If I hadn't had full control of her, the harsh glimpse she gave my uncut, bobbing dong would've pissed me off. I turned on the indirect lighting; because otherwise it'd be a sin to take and enjoy something this gorgeous and not look at it.

"Undress me."

That stubborn little bitch didn't move. When I repeated my order, she still didn't. I thought to change my approach, to physically force her or, fleetingly . . . to maybe let her go?

Shut the fuck up, Gran! You're not my conscience! No way I don't get *exactly* what I want out of *this one*, not out of one of Alex' most special women.

Especially, when I realized, right then, at that moment, looking at her unfettered beauty and resolute spirit, in re-playing how they'd so tediously chicken danced around each other earlier—she was "The One." Y'know. "The One" you change your worse behavior for. "The One" you "forsake all others for." "The One" you carefully woo and hopefully win, with enduring respect, because "The One" and only "One" is that nauseatingly precious to you.

And, he hadn't had her yet. Jackpot.

I grabbed the paw from my nightstand.

"Kara, undress me."

Before I'd put it down, she was reaching for me, undoing my shirt, stripping it from me. I watched her eyes. She didn't want to look in mine, nor did she want to look at me, so she closed them.

"Open your eyes."

She glanced up, full of sadness and anger, then stared forward at my hairy chest. I was especially pleased, when there was no coaxing needed nor hesitant fumbling while un-hooking my pants, though she did manage to pull them and my underwear down without directly focusing on the eager, angry dusk rose pink cock inches from her face. I'll fix that.

"Kiss me."

That was an intentionally loaded request, as she immediately began where she was, on my hairy thigh. When she tried to bypass my best buddy, I seized her by the hair and brought that exquisite face to my musky, aching crotch. I felt her neck stiffen, refusing me, as she pushed back against my hand, which vised her in place. The phone rang and the ancient machine picked up.

"Steve. It's Alex." She whimpered. I liked the sound. There was a considerable pause, then Alex simply stated, "You always could read people. I do . . . . I . . . love . . . Kara. I *want* her, *really* want her, desperately, but I don't want to fuck it up, like . . . well, *y'know*. That's all, good buddy. No, wait! Call me, leave a message. We should talk. Okay? See yah."

She sobbed, "Alex," almost inaudibly. Futilely. I shoved her beautiful face to my groin.

"You're kissing me." Her moment of hesitation was extremely brief. I *love* that hideous monkey. Her soft, full lips gently touched my sacs then proceeded up the underside of my rigid, thick cock. I momentarily considered having her suck my fat man off, but I wanted to be inside her, and see what Alex' virgin queen elect was like.

"Bed. Now."

She, finally, haltingly clambered onto my creaking antique brass bed—the very same one old Gran died in. Kara stared at the far wall, until I twisted her around to face me, which she plainly hadn't wanted to do. Her eyes. The fear was gone. No. It was suppressed, under her total contempt for me.

I kissed her, softly at first, then the lust kicked in, as I forced my tongue into her mouth. When I looked again, she had the same hate filled gaze for me.

Didn't matter.

"Lie back, open your legs." Her brow wrinkled with disapproval at my order, but she complied readily.

I moved between her thighs, and felt my erect and straining-to-play cock fall naturally against her cunt, and as it did so, I relished seeing her fear resurface. I didn't care if she didn't want me, she was getting me, as I slipped my dick's hard head between her musky, hairy lips. My balls cramped sharply with desire, as my glans met her slick cunt.

Oh yes, her mind and heart weren't in the game but her slippery cunt was. She stopped breathing awhile, as I slid past the defiant constriction of her inexperienced entrance and into her sweltering hole.

Mmm. Mmm. Good. *Tight* fit.

I pushed, and that snug, fallow length of pussy took me; until deep inside her, I met definite resistance.

Too damn good. "The One." And, a virgin.

Part of me wanted to viciously ram and rip the hell out of her, pound and batter the Mighty Alex' property to whimpering pieces like shattered wedding crystal, but instead, I steeled myself, restrained myself, by using . . . *Prince Alex' own trick, in his own words*—"for deflowering and multiple usage." I pulled nearly all the way out, then gently slipped back in, putting tender pressure on her "veil of purity," Gran called it, on the barrier of flesh and muscle constraining my access and protecting her physical virginity.

I patiently . . . maddeningly did this many more times, until, without a tear or drop of blood, I was rewarded, when her inner depths and juicy sweetness opened and yielded its deliciously forbidden fruit to me.

So did the smartest thought I've ever had.

I watched her eyes, because I knew she'd fight it. I touched the monkey's paw.

"Kara, make love to me . . . as if I were Alex."

A horrible scowl darkened her flawless beauty, making her more appealing. Several long moments passed before I felt her lovely body relax under me and her knees jerk up, shifting her pelvis up, then her thighs fell wider apart, opening . . . presenting the fresh pink inner depths of her engorged and ready, unspoiled sheath to me.

When she gazed at me again, it was the sparkling face she gave Alex, magnified by her unshielded desirous lust and love . . . for him.

Her ankles hooked around my legs, and . . . she fucked me. I fucked back.

She'd clearly given meticulous thought to how to pleasure Alex, while she melted my brain, as my nuts banged her crack without mercy. Like he'd said, she was "smart," "exceptionally capable," and making herself "absolutely indispensable."

She really put her heart into it.

It was quite nice being Alex. I glanced over at that hideously beautiful paw. It might be quite nice to remain her Alex, forever.

My Kara breathlessly came . . . her first with a cock . . . *my cock* buried to the hilt in her . . . most excellent. She came . . . tightly, furiously around my shaft, ankles hooked high up on my hips, as she whined sweetly, just like a little wild beast. She came in not so virginal multiple waves, which triggered me . . . making me cum hard, hot, and long, while I steadily pressed my cock into her, rocketing my searing spunk pointblank into her most unreachable depths.

A fucking explorer, first to land and leave his imprint on the pristine shore.

She shuddered intensely, lasciviously—milking me,

squeezing me entirely bone dry, as her sumptuous body remained arched against mine for another half minute, before she relaxed and let me go.

I didn't want to be free; especially, when I saw the fire still smoldering in her . . . for Alex. *Not me.*

No problem. This panting whore'd already entirely seduced me and spoiled me.

I'm staying that way.

Sorry, Alex.

* * * *

I left the indirect lights on dim, so whenever I'd open my eyes I'd see her there beside me. Even when she needed a bathroom break, I went with her and watched her, and "requested" she put her hands behind her head like a POW and spread her legs wide and do her business slowly, letting her hot, sweet water run over my hand. It was a joy watching her pee, because it was beautiful, but mostly because I enjoyed controlling her.

Controlling *his* her.

But, I must admit, all that domination and wishing and fucking—*sounds like an old British rock song*—made me hungry, so I let her sleep while I went fridge raiding for a sandwich and drink.

She didn't see me in the big chair, but I saw her, as she paused at her discarded, wet robe. She seemed incapable of both actions: of dressing *and* making it to the door. The door won. She touched the handle.

"Kara, come to me."

She frustratingly struck the door with her palms, as if to shove it out of her way, and sighed loud enough for me to hear her even at that distance, but she came; hips swaying, as only a woman's can, and her breasts . . . swaying and bobbing deliciously.

God, I am never letting her wear clothes again. Never. I may never let her out, period.

"P-Please . . . S-Steve . . . let me go." I almost gave it a thought. I almost felt for her. I gave her part of my sandwich, instead.

"Eat." She did. And, gave her drink. "Drink."

When she was done, I could see she was still waiting for my answer, which she got when I ordered her to get on her "knees and suck my cock, as if it were Alex'; and fill" her mouth with my cum.

She seemed distressed, which caused her naked breasts to heave wonderfully. But still, she got on her knees and said, "ah."

Y'know, nothing beats seeing and feeling your cock in the perfect pussy. Except perhaps two things: *seeing* your cod's big, tasty strawberry-shaped cockhead between the beautiful, flushed lips of a total stunner, especially one that belongs to your best friend, plus *feeling* her hot, wet mouth enwrapping tightly around you. Nursing on you. Drawing you in . . . and out . . . and in . . . and out.

She was doing an excellent job, even holding me correctly, so I wouldn't thrust too far into her little throat and choke her. I breathlessly asked if she'd sucked cock before, and got a muffled—.

"No."

I laughed, then asked if she'd imagined sucking Alex' cock, while watching porn movies or reading up on it at the library or through her Venus Book Club™ selections for pointers on the mechanics even.

The ill-tempered look on her perfect face said I'd hit it on the mark.

But, I wanted to hit something else, too, and commanded her to relax her throat and its gag reflex. I stood, held her pretty head steady by the hair, then pushed . . . making her swallow my *full*, fat length . . . until soft lips were pillowed in coarse, musky pubes.

I fucked Kara's hot, snug throat, as I instructed her to continue suckling my dearest, most in earnest buddy with her now well-educated lips and tongue.

She added a nice range of cum-calling hums on her own.

When my time neared . . . sensitive to my . . . to *Alex'* needs, she massaged and kneaded my destitute nuts with a pleasant hand, the perfect trigger. I readily came into the cozy, warm cup of her enthusiastic mouth. And, my cum *kept* cumming, balls and ass contracting sharply to shoot into her, until my well-used tool fell from those lips, until finally, her bright eyes on mine, I made her open.

My white lust lay to overflowing on her "*very* smart, exceptionally capable, absolutely indispensable, brilliant and innovative" pink tongue and pearly teeth, before I made her gulp down the best meal she'd ever had. My Kara licked the overflow off her lips and chin without prompting.

Creamy dessert.

That image alone could give me many hours of jerk off time in the future, but I'll have her, so I may never jerk myself again.

Poor Ole Spoiled Alex could get off completely on that same image, too, but he'll never see it.

Then, once again unprompted, Kara slurped and licked my glans and shaft, as if I were the sweetest bit of hard candy in the whole world. She playfully flicked her tongue's tip all over my cock's head and in my big snake's tiny mouth, until

I melted in her hands and slithered from her grasp.

* * * *

It didn't matter how late it was or how long we'd been at it, I had no desire to sleep and was entirely greedy for her, and she was greedy for . . . Alex. Lucky me.

I placed her on the dining table, and stood inside the open circle of her legs, as they wrapped around me. I started my meal at her mouth, working down, taking my time kneading and tasting both breasts and hard, sensitive nipple, then sat in a chair, her knees over my shoulders, parted her dark, silky pubes, and buried my happy face in her delicious, fragrant cunt.

I came up for air once or twice and checked her reaction. It'd been awhile since I'd touched the paw . . . .

Her expression was divided. Part of her plainly didn't want *me* eating her, and just as clearly she loved it, as she creamed all over me and moaned and wiggled reflexively, until seeming to give over fully to her lust again.

I considered asking her if she liked it because *I* did it so well or . . . because she was seeing and feeling me as Alex. I didn't though. I'm not fucking stupid. Instead, I instructed her to be as noisy as she wanted, that I wanted to hear her joy, as "Alex" kept his mouth to her, eating her succulent cunt out with a nasty vengeance.

Soon, her sometimes strained, sometimes husky, sometimes pleading voice was begging *him* to "lick harder," "nip" here, try a finger or tongue poke there . . . before crushing my head between her lustful thighs, while I drank her sweetly salty, hot stream of clear cum.

I love tasting *My* Sweet Kara . . . drinking *My* Sweet Kara. Fucking *My* Sweet Kara.

The next thing insured my wanting to fuck Kara forever.

I stood her up and turned her around, bending her over the old, mahogany, family dining table. I paused my huge, steel pillar over the tiny mouth of her little puckered shithole, but decided to save that still virgin entrance for tomorrow because I really wanted her sweet, new pussy again.

I again caressed and stroked the soft skin of her asscheeks with my cock, as she seductively waggled her tail side-to-side, enjoying the feel of me on her before arching her back so her wet, hairy snatch opened its plump lipped mouth to properly welcome and worship my rubberless length inside her.

I teased her slick burrow with my greedy arrow's tip and she glanced over her shoulder, eyes lustrous, full lips overflushed, and purposefully, hungrily, she pushed back to have me entirely in her. Her move came with a terribly appealing moaning sigh, as I slid home, making it hard to remember she'd been a fresh, untested virgin a mere few hours before, and was now the best cockhappy whore I'd ever had.

I laughed loudly, for joy, and enthusiastically fucked Kara like I completely controlled her. Which I did.

* * * *

I awoke when she got out of bed early.

"Where're you going?"

"Work?" I liked the way her statement became a question, waiting for my permission.

"No." I yawned and handed her the phone. "Call Alex—. His number at work. Say you won't be in, you're . . . staying in bed for the day."

She dialed, waited.

"It's Kara. I 'won't be in . . . staying in bed for the day'." Stilted, but it works.

She replaced the phone, and stared at the monkey's paw a long while. I touched it.

"Don't use it, ever. Come to me."

She slid her luscious body against mine, as if she actually meant it, which meant tons to me and is the greatest of aphrodisiacs, as I hardened immediately. She was still sore from the last hard fucking but was compliant and obedient, as I had her mount. There's nothing like watching a lover fuck herself on your granite, as she rode us both raw, riding me like a man should be ridden, which convinced me I should wish her . . . to love me, like she loved Alex . . . but . . . *instead of Alex*, and *always*.

* * * *

I half awoke, again, thinking . . . dreaming I'd heard shattering crystal glass, but . . . it was clearly nothing, so I fell back to sleep, spooned against the lovely and curvaceous Kara, until an incredibly strong hang viciously yanked me to the floor by the ankle. I landed painfully on my face, and someone stomped with purpose on my back, then booted me hard in the side.

Kara screamed, "Alex!"

He stopped. He looked entirely surprised that he had.

Good thing. I once watched him nearly beat a guy to death with his bare, hammer-hard fists. A guy, who'd attacked and hurt my sister. She says that's why she's always more concerned for Alex than me. Everyone's Charming Prince Alex, who was glaring at me, lying naked, doubled over at his feet, bleeding from my damaged nose and mouth, trying to get a decent breath around what had to be a deeply bruised and broken rib or two . . . or *three*. Stepping over me, he pulled the bed cover up to her, but she didn't take it. He took off his trench and buttoned her into it.

"Kara, what're you doing here?" Obvious question,

asshole, since she's completely tousled, reeking, and wearing absolutely nothing, except my cum.

"Making love with . . . Alex."

"*What?*" It seemed a good time for the paw.

It wasn't there!

Must've knocked it off when he pulled me down. I scrambled to look for it, since I knew I couldn't beat him in a physical fight, straight or dirty . . . or outrun him, with or without broken ribs. I wished I'd remembered that before having her call his new play toy, that'd mindlessly and automatically tagged my name and number.

Fuck. He was staring at me, seething, but got sidetracked when she amorously grabbed his crotch. He grabbed her disconcerting hand.

"W-What's wrong with you, Kara?!"

Shit! Shit! Shit! She pulled the bony paw out from under her pillow, and gave it to him.

"S-Steve . . . wished it." I knew he remembered Gran proudly showing it to him. Even senile, old chicks *love* Alex. He was flushing a deep vermilion on every bit of exposed skin.

I was so absolutely fuckin' dead, despite his trying hard to not look at me.

"What did Steve . . . wish for, Kara?"

I felt cold and distant, noticing, like you would details in a painting's composition at the art museum—how his head was tilted down in inner focus, and hers bowed too, almost touching his, but afraid to, as every word from that exquisite, cum-coated throat slit mine.

"'Make love to' him, 'as if' he 'were Alex'." It was interesting, her apologizing to him by her pleading tone and shrinking demeanor, as he asked her the questions he didn't want answers to, but asked anyway.

"How . . . how many—?" Hot tears rolled down her cheeks.

"F-Four . . . five?"

He didn't move, he was completely, totally still, which was unnaturally freaking my soul because Alex could move frighteningly fast and hard when he wanted to. Especially, when he was thoroughly, furiously pissed, like now. He never gets loud when he's severely angry. No, he gets deathly quiet . . . and still, as the eye of a furious tornado. Like now. Just before he explodes.

I realized I'd been painfully tensed all over, in anticipation of dying painfully, and tried to relax, thanking God she was present.

Kara'd changed Alex.

Of course, if she weren't present, I wouldn't be in fear of my life, blood leaking from me. Or libidinously sated.

"Why, Steve? You never believed in this damned thing."

I considered lying, but my brain was still Kara-fluxed—drinking her, fucking her—yeah, Kara-fluxed; I even had—Steve's Poe Paw, rhymes with faux pas—stupidly stuck in my head. But, I struck him to his ever too charming and all too self-centered soul with the simple, irreversible truth.

"I wanted her, Alex. Because she's, well, *look at her*. And, because *she's yours*, or . . . will be. Or, at least, would've been. You always get the best, then I get your dregs. *This time, you get mine.* Go. Take her. By the way, she's a totally wild, cocksucking, dickhungry, fuckcraving little whore—and I didn't even have to wish her to be. You can even fuckin' kill me, 'good buddy.' I don't give a shit, because *that* bitch's sweet, luscious cherry will *always* be mine."

Incredibly, Alex turned a deep berry color, but, more incredibly, he *didn't* slam my head into the wall. He was stone silent for a long time, then he looked at her.

She softly gasped—released.

He was holding the paw . . . and wishing her back to him!

Kara looked very confused, no—deeply shamed. It looked good on her incredible face; the perfect cum shot.

He held her face to his and whispered something to her, obviously trying to ease her agonized state, looked her deep in the eye, as if to see if she were truly mentally home, then kissed her, intensely. I thought, but didn't mention aloud, that I sincerely hoped he enjoyed the taste of my spunk on her lips and tongue.

I watched as that uncontrolled bitch hungrily kissed back, clinging to him, willingly giving him what I'd had to . . . .

I didn't like seeing that.

Fleeting thoughts crossed my mind, that if I could snatch the paw and wish before he kicked my balls into my brainpan, or if I could snap her beautiful neck before—.

He scooped her off my disheveled brass bed, sending her out ahead of him, making sure she was far out of earshot.

"Fuck the 'cherry' shit, Steve, and fuck you. When I'm done with it, I'm burning this damn thing to ash. All she'll ever remember, awake or in dreams, is *me* being with her, and all you'll remember is that *I'll fuckin' kill you,* in a way you *will* give a shit, if you *ever* come near her or me again."

* * * *

There. I always wake up *there,* from *The* Nightmare; my whole trembling body icy cold with fear and completely piss wet. I could never shake that horrible feeling once it came on, so I moved a good thousand miles away, years ago.

It's strangely funny, disturbing really, because before

moving, I awoke in my own house, in my own bed on freshly laundered sheets, with three broken ribs, a broken nose, and covered with many a bruise and dried blood; without any certain memory of how I'd gotten them or broken a glass door.

The strangest of all is that, once, when I was forced to go back there on business, I saw a stunningly gorgeous woman, who looked like the Kara in my . . . wet dream. She had a beautiful black-haired baby and . . . and I recall thinking how odd that her older, little boy looked so much like he could be mine.

But, I lost sight of them in the rushing traffic.

Silly. Just a silly coincidence and . . . wishful thinking. Dangerous wishes, somehow, although the strangest part of all is that I . . . I . . . don't . . . remember *ever* knowing an Alex . . . or a Kara. I most definitely, definitely hope I never do.

—oo—

more stories, scripts, and novel excerpts at

www.Neale-Sourna.com or **www.PIE-Percept.com**

Abbreviated version published—PLAYGIRL May 2002

Hesitation
[The Complete Short Story]
by Neale Sourna

I'd put off calling Tony for many months because . . . I was chicken. Completely Big Bird® yellow.

A brainy yet gorgeous man, who's nearly too handsome yet doesn't act it, a well-turned man, with a very neat, soft to touch, black musketeer/cowpoke mustache and goatee? An actor with a TV series, doing well in the ratings? (*Which all sounds a little too good, when you think about it. I do.*) I think a lot. Too much, I've been told, by practically everyone; except Tony.

I was "chicken," because, lately, just thinking about him made my walnut brown nipples too sensitive and my swollen, "dewing" crotch overly self-conscious. I couldn't stop thinking about him; I didn't want to.

"Sorry, my mind wandered," became my mantra at work and at the family's, as my mental and body arousing, Tony preoccupations became entire reveries. Long, wide awake, Technicolor™, dreamvisions of making love . . . fucking (*which is the same thing, with the right person*) with my touch-starved (*yet still particular about who touches it*) skin against his hot, masculine-scented, dark body.

Did I mention he has brains . . . "real" brains . . . and is a truly first-rate person . . . in a devilish way? Even my irreverently crazy family and friends love him—*all my favorite things in one man; scary, isn't it?*

Speaking of tongues, which we weren't, no one's ever kissed me better. I'd truly decided that electrifying kisses were only in fiction and other women's lies; so, what would I come to, if he ever got his softly whiskered, gently insistent lips and hot, articulate tongue down onto my peek-a-boo, light mulberry-shaded clit?

My problem? Well, my dreams and mind, when all alone, have taken my body to . . . great ecstasies, yet my same body has ALWAYS choked, in the clinches of unsatisfying "real" sex.

In younger years, some of it was uneducated inexperience, misinformed by fictional hype and just being afraid to . . . let nature run its wild course . . . when a man like Tony, or not so like Tony touched me. But, not all of it was in my mental head.

Doctors really don't know everything. When puberty struck, about age nine, I'd get tingly just sitting next to a boy, then something . . . . I stopped tingling; skin, cunt, hell, I couldn't feel my own tits. Well, I could feel them, but my body felt like I was being touched through a thick, Cleveland winter coat—some pressure but no excitement. That lack of physical arousal overtook me, without warning and stayed for many, many years. No matter the guy or my love interest.

However, this past year and a half, since getting Tony chronically on the brain, despite eluding him, my physical . . . malady has, just as mysteriously, left me. Masturbation aside, for me, getting wet, staying aroused or climaxing with a man, or simply getting two fingers comfortably inside me, let alone a man-sized dick . . . had always been a problem. No matter how I tried to "relax," "let go," "try harder to get into the feel," or other such advice drivel. Usually male.

(Sorry, I bitch.)

Which all means, I was past overdue for a good fucking and really hoped I had a chance of getting something out of an intimate relationship besides feeling I'd been merely sterilely hugged. If I were going to fail again, after a riderless . . . decade out of my disappointing saddle, I decided I wanted to fall from the high, strong back of this particular, blue-ribbon prized stallion. So, I'd choked up my nerve and phoned Tony, who sounded glad to hear from me and didn't mock search his mind and say, "Neale? With an extra 'e'?" Instead, he . . . squealed.

(Don't mention "Deliverance" or I'm stopping this tale right here.)

He sounded like he was trying to contain himself, and was "very glad" I called and "would be more than happy to meet" me at Piggy's on The Square.

He arrived first, in the unexpected, light rain, despite my

being quite early—in my attempt to acclimate myself before his arrival. Piggy's, unfortunately, had a sudden kitchen sewage flood and was closed for the night. It, also, abruptly downpoured and was a long way back to his car. *(Mine was in the shop and all the cabs were . . . elsewhere.)*

Plus, the Square is wide open, without awnings. We got soaked, and it got cold. I'm lousy, healthwise, when I'm soaked and cold, and was considering that my girlfriend was right about "coincidences" and that "water means emotions."

(But, does that mean sewers mean deep, dirty, or backed up emotions? Or rain means heavenly emotions? Or, that my emotions were an uncontrolled mess, and "acting out in physical form" . . . disintegrating my world; making me a drenched pussy, no longer dressed to impress, with nowhere to go, except back home?)

Home, however, was cut off by flooded streets, downed powerlines, and police cruisers warding us off; therefore, the road to spare clothes and warmth at my gallery,

"Neale's . . . ALL NUDE Photos and Prints",

a few blocks from home was also off limits. *(There's a sweetly nasty, old couple, who come in biweekly to call me a filthy pornographer. I get new stock biweekly.)*

Anyway, I was trembling, Tony was afraid I'd "freeze and shatter into bits, like freeze-dried coffee," and suggested taking me to the only safe, dry, no dress standards place that wasn't off limits—his place. I sighed. Deeply. Not only was I now poster girl for "Les Miserables", but my slinky "dry clean only," now-embarrassingly-stuck-to-me, silk blend outfit had died.

(Did I mention the snappy yuppie sedan that doused us both, especially me? A girl could get a complex, or something.)

Plus, I was on my way to the homebase of the one man *(whose charmeuse shirt and linen slacks were sticking to him quite nicely),* who made me so aroused and nervous, I could practically puke, or faint. Or both. How attractive and erotic is that?

* * * *

Tony's new place suited him; masculine but not annoyingly so and smelled nice, instead of like a men's dorm or locker room with that awful, horrid reek not unusual to other's of his species' dwelling places. He contemplated what I could change into; his sister had been staying over, but was gone now, and hadn't left anything useful behind; besides, we were "very different body types, anyway."

(Which he said in a very complimentary manner.)

He'd been thinking out loud, while rubbing my arms and back, as my chilled trembling shifted to slightly aroused trembling. I was glad he couldn't see my face. *(Oh, geez, a mirror!)*

"Gotta get you out of these sopping clothes, Neale. You're not warming up fast enough."

"That's what all the men say." Oh. I say stupid things when I'm erotically stressed. Tony looked at me *(still a charmer, even drenched in acid rain)* and silently, teasingly waggled his brows. Smart man, keeps his oddball comments to himself. *(I really have to learn that.)*

"I'll get you something of mine to wear, if you don't mind." *(Mind, mind, why would I mind?)* I mutely nodded, as he showed me the bathroom.

I'm not a shower person, but I was so cold, I stripped right away and jumped in. I also forgot the door was cracked open, he'd meant to come right back, but his phone rang. He talked, evidently on a cordless, as his voice moved room to room, while I rinsed off crud and date makeup—he might as well see the real me, instead of smudged me. I was still a little chilled in the warm shower fog, then realized shutting out the door draft would help, when he bopped in with a robe for me; wearing only a change of boxer briefs.

(I noticed "a change," because they were dry, except where touching his rain dampened, delightfully lumpy, and becoming lumpier, masculine places.)

I stared. He stared. Until. I realized he had more to stare at than I did; he realized it too, and slipped out of the briefs. *(I had a quick inner vision of passing out, hitting my head, and missing everything, yet being very happy in self-inflicted death with what I'd seen of him.)*

But, like my Mom's old Peggy Lee record sang, "I thought I'd die, but I didn't©," as he stepped in with me. We . . . awkwardly, laughingly maneuvered around each other, as he rinsed off, while endeavoring to never take his eyes off me. And vice versa. Becoming self-conscious, I stepped back. He pulled me to him and I felt his penis, like hot stone against my belly—a sensation, which I most definitely felt, nearly stopped my heart, as blatant desire for him radiated through me, and his wonderful mouth clamped on mine, short-circuiting my ever too busy brain. Maybe it was too much oxygen, from when my breathing changed.

Pleased with my arousal, he continued giving me his full attention, as his warm, strong, soap-lathered hands caressed me. Occasionally, he'd rub his body against mine. When his attentions were becoming too much . . . he rinsed me. I wanted to touch him in turn but held back . . . .

(I'm an obsessive hesitator, until I eventually let go; then— BAM! I'm also an idiot, I was already naked and skin to skin with the object of my desire . . . yet . . . . Maybe a lobotomy . . . ?)

He noticed my . . . indecision or he was just craving me to touch him, and whispered in my ear . . . his hot breath and spectacular voice boring inside my mind.

"Wash me."

I thought of that same message finger-scribbled on dirty vehicles and mentioned it. *(I was stalling.)* He took my finger to invisibly stencil those words across his gently hairy, broad chest, then handed me the shampoo.

We had to laugh, at a point, because there was far too much lather everywhere, as I made foam creatures out of him, while he'd splatter me with suds. But, when I abruptly became serious, and finally stroked his balls and magnificent dick with my soapy, lustful palms . . . we rinsed off.

His penis bumped heavy against the small of my back and top of my sensitive ass cheeks. He turned off the distracting water, with its obscuring steam, as I used the tiled wall to support my "weak at the knees" symptoms. Tony stooped, and I instinctively raised up on my toes, as he pushed his smooth cockhead between my thighs, wetting himself in my lust. He moved between my swollen labia, to press deliciously against my clit, while his fingers combed through my pubes to massage my hairy mound . . . giving me . . . sensation from both sides.

His cock moved back until my hungry, slippery cunt, without hesitation, gasped open to have him and I purposefully stepped back. My snug, yet, eager welcome pleased him. None of me resisted him, and he slid inside me, as I took him. *(No fuss, no muss.)* I felt his beautiful cockhead drag, full length, along the newly sensitive, slick, muscular walls of my vagina.

(It scared me! I adored it!! I'd never felt . . . . And, I'd, frankly, never liked the sound of a man panting and growling over me, until . . . him.)

He nearly pulled out of me. *(I'd've cried or bitched very loudly, if he had.)* Even the vacuum his dick's absence left felt . . . divine. He pushed in, a bit at a time. A little in. A little out. A little . . . deliciously around. And around.

(I . . . love . . . screwing.)

He pushed on my G spot, again, outside and in, as I held his hand there and shoved and screwed back to have him completely inside me. He pumped and whispered to me, making me whimper for wanting him even more, before he became still, steadying himself against the misty wall tiles, as I, unrestrainedly, hardfucked back against him and his throbbing, very alive cock.

(Fucking was never like this. I . . . love . . . fucking Tony!)

I finally strained against him, clutching a deep growl from him, until his white lava and my own hot lust waters flowed from me.

We bear-hugged. His hard cock was still in me, as his words, also, penetrated me.

"I love you, Neale." I remained still; my body'd already answered.

—oo—

Novella excerpt from short story collection — work in progress:

LIBIDINOUS 1:
Erotic Exercises

featuring

Grant's Boone
by Neale Sourna

. . . Grant smiled, her lips overflushed and inviting, her voice husky from the activity.

"Do you want more, Boone? More of me? If you do, you should figure out who else you can call."

She wiped her lip of a stray drop of creamy cum then

sucked it off her thumb, before perching on his desk, her shapely legs crossed, her skirt high on her firm thighs showing the pink lace atop her thigh-high stockings, as she polished off his bottled water with a seductive lick. He rubbed his mouth with the weight of this new offer clearly delighting him. He was losing his pokerface, and his dick lay naked and exposed in his lap. She waited, and stared out the window at what little you can see at such an oxygen rare height as this.

He requested his executive assistant, VQ, to call a certain judge, a highly respected and extremely well placed jurist, who was away but who would be back in twenty minutes or so. Boone instructed Quartermain to remain on the line for the judge and that he would be emailing documents for the judge's immediate attention. Boone didn't bother to put his cock away as he took the disk Grant had brought, with copies of all her supporting files, reloaded it, and sent its contents through.

While they waited, he used his control system to obscure the windows and lock his door. He turned on the indirect lighting, including that over his hardwood, conference table, stood and hooked a hand under her knee, uncrossing her legs.

He pulled her head to him and kissed her, she kissed back. What he wanted, she let him have. So, he sucked her lip and her tongue, then moved down to her breasts. She let him have those as well, as his one hand explored the smoothness of her outer thigh, to that special woman's roundness, the underside of her hip, and, from the back and beneath, found the crotch of her silk and lace panties.

Boone rubbed until they were sopping wet then his burning hand slid under the cloth, his fingers slipping between the swelled, torrid lips of her sex, and slipped his middle and ring fingers as far as they'd go inside her. He bit and pulled gently on a mouthful of breast as he pulled out his fingers then rammed them back deep into her. He heard her breath catch and felt her tighten around his fingers.

She pushed him out of her and made him release her tit. She was breathing heavily, trying to stay in charge, although he could clearly see she was becoming very smoky and wanting mor—.

"No more, Boone. If the judge gives you what I want, then you get what you want."

"Well, I want a lot. What's to stop me from taking it, right this moment?"

"The game. You like the game. We both like winning, but if we both lose this one, you'll figure you got this close and that you'll get me the next time."

"It's already been two years, I don't want to wait till 'next time'."

There it was again . . . that overtly potent urgency of his. Could any woman really satisfy hunger like that? Her girlfriends from the old neighborhood would beat her shitless for stopping to think, let alone having already passed up a number one prize, married or not, like Boone Hutchinson. Grant's comeback to that erred opinion was that, that was exactly why I left the old neighborhood as soon as I could, in the first place. And, go back as seldom as possible.

Boone's want was awakening that fear he always seemed to arouse in her, so she put on her best game face and pretended she was fearless.

"I . . . really don't care. You're not wanting to wait, means nothing to me. Not unless there's "something," and you know what, "in it" for me. Or, should I say, my client. You break this judge, your puppet judge breaks your puppet politician, and I'll break your balls, no further strings attached. Capice?"

"Very capice. You came in here a little timid but you're

making up for it just fine. Nothing like having your opponent's dick hanging out his pants just waiting—?"

VQ put the judge through. The judge had gotten the evidence, the speakerphone barked. It made sense but again more hemming and hawing and another set of cold feet. Grant put Boone's hand between her hot thighs and he slipped again into her panties and into her, she shut her legs tightly around him, with a look of "what are you going to do, now."

Boone was, if nothing else, a man who could think straight and true under pressure, especially when something was between him and what . . . who he wanted. He insisted. The judge balked, but Grant kept Boone's hand in her, as she leaned to his ear and whispered, hotly and with purpose.

"I want my client out. Free. Tonight. By midnight. It's doable. Your judge is just bullshitting. Even a nonlegal person can see that. *I want this done now*. And, I want you inside me within the next five minutes. Can you handle that, or are we done here?"

His only thought for about five seconds was, "This bitch is busting my balls in the worse way," and that he appreciated her tactics.

"Judge, are you alone? Take me off speakerphone, would you."

[more]

LIBIDINOUS 1:
Silver Pole
(from Libidinous 1)

. . . G'd left for a last minute upscale, bachelor party, when Max, I - Am - An - Ass - And - *Completely* - Spineless, said Dark had finally "requested" I dance for him. Yes, Max made finger quotes.

I'd asked Ginger once if she liked dancing for Dark. She giggled. Remember, with G, giggling means me . . . or money. Translation, she doesn't like men but she'd even fuck him, since he pays well. He'd better because I can charge more than the others. I get the patrons to come inside, and bring their friends, and I keep them all there longer and cumming right here in my hot, little hand.

I really considered not dancing for that imperiously bossy snot though.

But, maybe I'm stupid, because Dark's sudden interest in a private dance, after ignoring me, except for my general dances and to taunt me backstage, had me a smidge . . . intrigued.

Well, actually, more than a smidge.

* * * *

He didn't want me on his lap, so I and my delicate, gold Egyptian bracelets gyrated and twisted, and displayed and fingered and shook my more obvious assets from a distance.

He seemed pleased, while Shadow [his huge bodyguard] looked on. Minutes later, Shadow put down lots of Mr. Franklins. I guess, his boss didn't want to get his hands dirty. I was reaching for the loot.

"Again."

"They're your Bennies," I said.

This close to him, this long, it was starting to get to me that he never looks at me like anyone else does. Not like his Shadow, who was trying hard *not* to look at me. I know when a man's looking at me, and Shadow'd lost the battle. The hard proof being the growing precum stain, from his stiff billy club in his pants that he tried to modestly shift to a more comfortable position.

Unless, of course, he had a big thing, for his boss.

"Come here."

The sahib indicated I may now approach, and buff his lap, which I did thoroughly. The song ended. Shadow piled on the Poor Richards.

"Again," said Dark. The Greedy bastard.

He peeled off his long, stylish jacket. A little warm, I guess. Y'know, others want lots of dances, too, but they don't have the cash or credit, or they're afraid they'll cum their slacks. Dark seemed to be holding his cream but his trousers were becoming less slack the more I rode his very expensive imported, custom tailored fabric.

Then, he touched me.

"*No touching!*"

I'd dismounted so fast, I don't think he'd expected it. The look on his face said touching me was no overinfatuated mistake. As *they* always say.

Tiny Natalie'd had some queer lick her ass just yesterday.

Totally creepzoid.

We do a lot. But, it's a *service,* a *special service,* and it has its limits. Let's face it; we're vulnerable—naked, outweighed, unarmed, with help far enough away that we could get seriously damaged or dead before the bouncers get to us.

So, touching me . . . us is very much breaking the law. And, *my* law.

Most people still like to think we're wearing pasties or nude plastic or Sally Rand feathers, "if these kinds of places must exist," they say. But, no, the law says nude's—fine, opening my legs—fine, touching myself or another performer's anything is—fine, but . . . customers touching us . . . me is forbidden. As I rub my body against theirs.

I'm on . . . I *am* that *thin, fragile* line between voyeurism and participation, stripping *(Since I'm naked, I strip your mind, not my clothes.—Good, huhn?)* and prostitution.

"Dez, it was just your waist I touched."

"It doesn't matter, Dark. *You touch nothing.*"

"All right. I'll behave. Finish. Please?"

I didn't like the look in his eyes, I couldn't read it, and, the pit of my stomach churned. Never a good sign.

"If you want more, Dez . . . . A penalty fee?"

Where was Shadow pulling those bills from?!

He never put his hand in a pocket, no bill fold or wad seemed to be in his huge hand, and then *Blam!* He put down ten of them this time, for his master; fanned so I could count.

"You're not stupid, Dez, you know I like you. I just momentarily forgot proper decorum."

"Bullshit." He smiled at my anger, which pissed me good.

"Okay. One last dance. You get paid, and I'll go. I'll never come back here to Max', unless you give me permission."

I had to think about that one.

The money was better than great, and there'd be more, he always pays, even if he only watches for thirty seconds. And, then his royal pain in my ass would leave . . . he could dry hump himself.

I wished he'd stop looking like he knew exactly what I was thinking, which, of course, I knew he did.

So, I Salome'd again, and he asked me to straddle him, which is not unusual, especially from a high-paying client. I mounted him and his eyes held mine for a long time, his prodigious bulge between my legs, throbbing deliciously, making my bare pussy dampen it's tongueless mouth. I tried to move off the expensive fabric . . . before I—.

"Wet it, Dez, I don't care."

How'd he know I was getting so wet? I thought to disobey, but I liked the constant throb his cock was singing to my cunt. I wanted more. He could tell.

"Put your hands on my shoulders, and lean into me."

I hesitated, but finally did it, and it felt *wonderful*, but I was loosing control, and the position put his hot lips too close to my breasts. If I'd been flatterchested we would have stayed within the law, but my tit brushed his hot mouth and he grabbed me and sucked. Lighting a flash fire from my cunt to my brain.

Pulling away made him suck harder, biting just a bit, and his pants got wetter, at least from my side.

He smiled, mouth full of me, knowing he had me, knowing he was getting my body, that's controlled by me, that serves me, to betray me.

I pulled away to dismount, and his teeth let go but he held me on his hard bulge, pushing it up into me. I wanted it, but I wasn't having it, as I shoved to get away. He grabbed a handful of hair on the back of my head.

Piss me! Tryin' to <u>control</u> me.

I backhanded him, and, suddenly, he had a switchblade at my ribs.

"She's thinking whether or not I want her enough not to slice her beautiful body, or if I'm afraid someone might hear her call out, and come for her." He pulled my head to his. "Delectable Dez, who's going to run through *that* door and into *him*? And, if they got past him, who'd run up on *me*?

Even for you."

"What d'you want?"

"Control of you."

Thought so.

I elbowed him in the neck.

He let go.

I screamed and made a break to pass the huge guy, who moved faster than a guy his size usually does. I think he's made out of granite, too. And, by the way, I didn't hear any help coming.

Goddamn that mouthbreathing Max.

I knew it was stupid from the start, but I kept going anyway, and turned around. Dark was able to inhale and swallow again. Scarily, he'd let me go, but the knife'd never left his fingers, which it did now, as he threw the blade point into the floor.

At least he really didn't want to cut me.

I ran past him to the other door, a sometime dressing room/stage exit. I never made the exit, as he pinned me with his hard body, titside, to the cold wall.

"Let's talk, Dez, or rather you listen. Your buddy Ginger's working a *very* private party. *I'm* throwing *that* party, so I can have this one, with you, without her overprotective and intrusive interference. Which all means, that I know you, that you'd probably let me hurt you, just to not *obey* me, therefore, *you will obey me* or it'll be one call, one word from me, and she'll discover the unspeakable joys of a gang bang."

Damn. I couldn't even hit him with an elbow or knee.

"You're insane."

He ran his hand down my bare curves and behind, then slipped his long fingers deep inside me. My gasp wasn't because it hurt.

"No. I just get what I want. And, you know exactly what I want from you."

He removed his probe to smell and taste me off his fingers, let me go, and sat down. He pulled the blade out of the floor and put it away.

"You're taking too long, Dez. Unzip me and mount up. *Now*."

He smiled in that too annoying, owns - the - whole - fucking - world . . . and - you - too way of his, knowing I took direct orders very badly, but, because of G, that I was taking *this* one.

I went to him . . . .

[more]

LIBIDINOUS 1:
Tenure [M/M/M]
(from Libidinous 1)

I was about a month deep into my first Tenured Semester, my mind going as lukewarm and flat as the stale champagne in my glass, while the University President and his usual asskissers continued to mutually stroke one anothers' swollen egos about . . . I have no idea. I'd tuned out long ago after their profusely embarrassing thank you's to me for the mega income I'd generated for the school with my last award winning publishing and was steadily edging my way to the back, as I picked up a scotch rocks on my way out.

I'd leave altogether, but it might seem a little obvious, so I decided wandering around the Presidential Mansion would kill time, fewer brain cells, and give me a tenable cover should any of the Faculty or one of the especially invited Freshmen blurt, "Hey, where'd you go, Professor?"

I saw the seeable sights of donated artworks and furniture in this wing and decided crossing over to the far side wing had merit. I had the entire place to myself and took my time scrutinizing the antiques that hadn't been taken out for storage yet.

Then, I heard him.

It's a pretty unmistakable sound—moaning gasps like that, underlined by a rhythmically repeated squishy slap sound that called my curiousity. Another deeper male voice randomly counterpointed, and the antebellum floorboards squeakily accented everything.

The songs of Sirens calling me . . . from around the next open double doorway.

His face was locked in concentration, feral eyes half-closed, as he moaned and "panted prettily"; got that from an old Linguistics roommate, who was, of course, fascinated with words and phrases. Never had a use for it, until now.

Recognized him. A Freshman of beautifully blended, slightly exotic, indeterminate ethnicity. The kind male and female professors lose their jobs over and other Students get pitched out on their ear for. Zil was on his knees—elegant palms on the wine red carpet covered wood floor, elbows bent, shoulders down, ass up, totally naked, his young, slim golden body rocking, forward and back—getting his bunghole thoroughly whacked, which was something I'd academically, continuously wet dreamed about since the first time I'd seen him.

The lucky whacker had his long, dark, curlyhaired head down, fully concentrating on Zil's tail, as the antique floor creaked under the weight of their indulgences.

Zil looked up at me, clearly he saw me and just as clearly didn't care. Both of them were beautiful; Zil disturbingly prettily, but his lover was harder cut and perfect at every angle.

His dark caramel tanned body was a Classic Greek's wet dream of a god, although I still couldn't see anything of his face. That was probably classic and perfect, too. I'm not, so, I really notice good lines, and true beauty. I've got decent height, but I'm body and face by Mack™ truck, more Bob Hoskins than Keanu Reeves.

The old mansion music parlor had only one piece of furniture left in it; a tufted piano stool. Fascinated, I commandeered it into the perfect line of sight of his . . . perfect arrow shaft pounding in and out of Zil's oil slicked, golden valentine. By the way, that is where the heart shape for St. Valentine's Day comes from. It doesn't look like anyone's actual chest pump so much as a man's favorite view of his lover's sweetest erotic angle. Trust me on this fact, I teach Culture and Mores.

Don't laugh, or I won't finish my tale.

I sipped my scotch watching young Zil's rigid dick beating time to the music of his incredible ass banging back against the other, who leaned into Zil, furiously walloping in return. The godling's face was up, thrown back at an angle that still hid it from view, and I had to shift to take the pressure off my own distending nads.

Then both pretty darlings before me blew, hard, as their crotches arched strongly together, their young balls shaking severely. Zil had his head down, his entire body quaking, dickhead pinched tight in his hand, darkened to the color of ripe, fresh fruit before bursting. I again shifted on my perch, as he wiggled and got a yelp out of the one behind him, who quavered and spurted the last of his cum into Zil's sweet, receptive anus, as Zil bore down and recklessly gushed his milk onto the red, antique carpet.

David—*I decided to name my young godling for that great Italian statue*—leaned forward and slipped his arm around Zil's slim waist, face still hidden, and spoke in his lover's ear.

Oddly, watching Zil stretch and rub his body against David's like a lithe bronze cat, for some reason, almost made me blow my wad in my shorts. Then, David kissed Zil's neck, shoulder, and slapped him, hard, on his superb ass.

I was right about David's face. Every line and tight pore was perfect.

They completely ignored me as they dressed, as only the young can; even while naked, so I snapped my fingers. It's a trick I stumbled across with my own kids. The loud snap always got their attention, and annoyance once they realized I snapped for the dog as well.

Both deigned looked my way, plainly finding me amusing; Zil also found the gaze I gave him a challenge, and headed my way. Damn. A breathtakingly beautiful man-child, and still mostly naked; the only thing he'd put on was a tee top. Young David laughed at me, but this was my break and I don't blow chances as special as this.

Zil, smelling like sex, came close enough for me to touch him, so I did, starting at the inside of his firm, smooth thigh, and up and deep, feeling his lax cock on the back of my hand, as I ignored it to caress his nads, before following the ridge there back, as I rubbed my finger near his still oiled joy hole. He let me touch whatever I wanted. I took my sweet time touching everything. I have large, strong, gentle fingers. I've been told that more than once.

You make beauty when you don't have it.

Young Zil wasn't complaining, as I coaxed him closer, with my finger pressuring his nuts and his shithole simultaneously, my hot palm pressuring and warming his p-spot, but he'd just had his sweet bum blasted thoroughly by Young David over there, so I had to make my point.

Kids don't listen.

You have to show them your authority. Then they'll listen.

I removed my fingers, smelled, then poured some of my iced scotch on Zil's young cock, making him gasp with the chill, before I smartly stroked the length of him, and lightly flicked my fingertip across his sensitive glans. David was already forgetting I existed; however, I now had Zil's full attention.

Zil said, "More."

Pretty and a pig. Perfect. He turned so my grip on him would be better, as I kept stroking him and the youth went steel hard in my hands, as I poured the last of my drink, anointing him, chilling him, then rewarming him with my hot palm.

I unzipped.

I saw David past Zil's ass, watching us, completely dressed except for long stroking his flawless peter. A Kentucky Derby thoroughbred. However, when mine tumbled out into my large mitt, in its eagerness and enlarged to its full thickness and length, that caught *his* full attention. Clydesdale. "In the house," as my annoyingly young Students say. I have in fact been told, even by men in sports showers, that my cock is my beauty.

Wonderful, the one part of me not exactly available for perpetual, open display.

I saw lust in David's eyes and one particular thought flew into my brain; a very distracting thought. Having them both . . . ?

END OF EXCERPT

www.Neale-Sourna.com
or www.libidinous.neale-sourna.com

Libidinous@neale-sourna.com

Novel excerpt, work in progress:

Aegis
[ee'-jis]
A Fable of Sexual Control, Compulsion, and Release

by Neale Sourna

. . . I left alone for Gina Torres' place, where torrid, gracefully energetic men can dance or at least try to, and it's at a heart-thumping speed and decadence, so a girl can shake all her horny shit. Then, Guy *[pronounced ghee, in the French manner]* was there, too. Looking like he fucking owned the place and everyone in it.

Gina dearest would beg to differ.

He didn't seem at all out of place; but, then again, Gina's is a pretty upscale place.

Guy's whole relaxed, still bearing stated, "I can do something for you no other man here can."

He'd danced quite a bit earlier, at the Chief's birthday party, once with me and most notably without, until the haughty wives' and girlfriends' fawning over his gorgeous fine ass—*let's face it, he's a fair identical twin for handsome and talented actor/martial artist Russell Wong of "Romeo Must Die"*—had got in the way of his clearly keeping tabs of me.

Then, the Arabella disappearance.

He wasn't dancing here at all. When a man's body moves as expertly as his, it's okay if he conserves vital, potent energy for bagging his prey and I was very tired of being pawed by talentless amateurs.

I worked my way to the club's rooftop, knowing my favorite Cerberus, Che, would stop him on the stairs.

The roof is off limits.

Che is Gina's cousin and likes me.

I like him, too; he's a darling teddy bear, who takes good care of his mother, his grandmothers, and helps with his sister's boy. He's a real sweetie . . . too much so in fact, which translates to too good for me.

No, really. He'd let me destroy him.

And, I would, because I could.

Dearest Che deserves . . . better than . . . me.

A few minutes later, Guy was on the roof. *Sounds like that joke about breaking the news of a death in the family, with the brother's dead cat and then his mama being on the roof.*

If you're not a very hot chica, who makes Che's job interesting, the only way to get on the roof during business hours is to pay him beyond handsomely. *Nice to know Guy's not cheap with the folding Gouda.*

Guy found me, in the chilled night, walking, dancing actually, to the pounding beats from downstairs of Lenny Kravitz' "Fly Away". I was walking along the roof wall's edge. Guy spoke. He's got a very pleasantly mellowy clear voice.

"I'd heard, among many things, that you were fearless . . . and crazy."

He asked me to come down to him. Chivalrously—*Or was it just an excuse to touch me?*—he handed me down, then slipped his expensive suit jacket on me. Then, I jumped back up on the ledge. I'm a bit perverse in that way. I don't like orders from people, who haven't proved their authority, particularly an LT [lieutenant].

I asked if he were . . . "in love" with me already, or couldn't wait to spill out his "yearning desire" and "sweet tenderness" all over me. I'd been hearing that kind of crap all night. No. Really.

And, some of it . . . a LOT more nauseatingly florid.

He scrutinized me a long time with his so root beer brown?, laughing brights—*judging what I wanted for an answer, most likely.*

"No. Little Girl, I just want to fuck you."

Good answer. A very good answer. But, no "pass go", yet, Buddy.

"I thought, maybe, you wanted to fuck Arabella." He smiled, almost sheepishly . . . almost. *His eyes puff and crinkle in a neat way at the outer corners.*

"Young Ms. Gaines is a brat. Brushed against me and believed my growing hard-on was for her; said she could . . . 'take care' of it for me. So, I suggested a little taste test."

Goddamnit. I want, no, *need* this dick . . . and this fucking penishead's got Chief Gaines' daughter on her spoiled, bony ass knees sucking his cock. He smiled like he knew exactly what I was thinking.

"Weak technique, weak tongue, no throat or gag control, no fucking skill whatsoever. Didn't even know what to do with her hands. Wasn't worth the time it took to slip on the rubber, and tire out her jaws . . . not with you in serious heat out here.

"Artemis, you seen the type, always pushing up on a man, like she knows what to do with him. And doesn't. Figured a man-sized cock stuffed down her immature gullet would shut her the fuck up. Give her something to tell her Spelman sorority sisters, once the sore throat's gone and her voice returns."

I was getting impatient about getting hold of his "man-sized cock" and was still standing above him on the wall, when I let him touch me, with one hand. If a man can't get you going with the minimum: a look, a word, one hand, or tongue, then he won't be able to deliver the rest.

Guy chose well, and directly. His hand slid up between my knees and turned to stroke both hot, smooth thighs, until he found my "silken-haired"—Stosh's phrase.—pantyless crotch. I was already breathing a little too deeply, and sopping wet, had been all night, knowing he and his brother were circling, doggedly pursuing me.

I was definitely feelin' it.

His fingers knew what they were doing, as my snatch ached sharply and I closed my legs tightly around his gently rude digits, which he thrust up, deep into me . . . thumb pressing increasingly, mercilessly on my swollen clit.

Simple things; but, *soooo many get it wrong.*

Exceptional. I so wanted more than a few long phalanges, and abruptly pushed him out of me. I could see his digits glistening in the night, covered with my wet, which he took his time smelling, as if committing my scent to memory, before sucking the taste of me off them.

He purposefully, teasingly walked away, as I jumped down, in pursuit, and unzipped him. He watched as I reached in, and pulled out a weighty, well-heated, swelling . . . and lengthening, prime alpha boner, that my eager, little hand immediately—.

The bastard snatched it from me, pushing me against the brick wall, up onto the little step—which has I'm not sure what practical purpose other than equalizing our heights nicely. Those eyes. Medium brown. Root beer or . . . . *God, what ingenious shade(s) is that?* They darkened with lust and scrutinized every centimeter of my face, then trailed down, before dawdling with his information gathering palms at my breasts. In his pleasant preoccupation, I'd slipped my hand back around that exposed, upright beauty of his, and its two extraordinary, sweating and ready for sport companions. His hands dropped to hold onto my waist, as his eyes half closed while I stroked.

Damn. You could dance by the strong, pulsing beat throbbing in that motherfucker.

He suddenly looked at me, before yanking up the front of my dress. His nose flared, filling with my aroused scent, as he audibly sighed, appreciatively, and so did I when his fingertips lightly stroked my humid bush. I simply don't believe in little sculptured pubic patches or childlike, hairless cunts. I'm not a goddamn Italian gardener . . . or a damn child.

If you want a woman, who looks like one . . . and fucks like one, you come to me. And this motherfucker was stalling.

"You said you wanted to fuck me. So . . . fuck . . . me."

For an LT, most of whom couldn't find their own soft, inward-drawn, tiny dicks on bright, sunny days, he took orders well. He clasped hard onto me, as he took literal physical possession of my bare ass and dove; plunging up into the deep end, deliciously smashing me back into his custom-made jacket, snagging it against the prickly, biting bricks.

God, I love the cologned scent of this man, and . . .

. . . I love the way a man's cock, no matter what size to near bursting outside of a cunt, swells even more upon contact with Grade A pussy. I'd been more than right about Lieutenant Guy Fellowes, a true prince of purple royalty and positively Olympic gold. Excellent, because I really was in no mood for coy, gentile, intramural soft . . . ball.

When I'm like this, and I'm more often like this than I

care to say, it's Big Show hardball or nothing.

And, that was certainly not "nothing" I had hard and alive and feverishly buried deep between my hungry thighs, his pants rubbing against the soft skin inside them. He paused a while, my sweet cunny having a damn good grip on him, as he pulled up one of my legs ever so high, to deliciously slowly push even deeper into me. I'd . . . I'd never felt any man throb so hard . . . like *that* . . . inside me . . . .

Breathtaking.

[story break]

Let's just say I was feeling very mean.

She'd stood out pale and still and very out of place on the active dance floor, in that diversely colorful crowd and the same could be said when Cassie followed me to my roof. Well, Gina's roof. My temperature was already running too hot on a chilly night, my pink leather jacket cast aside, as I lay on my precarious, cold, stone ledge, nearly exactly where Guy'd come to me that first night.

I was feeling the driving beats from the dance floor below coursing through me, and I startled her when I asked what she wanted. Not what the Hell she wanted, merely *what* she wanted.

"Ren." Wow, she's so very much come to the wrong person.

"Well, Cass, since he and Guy both cut my name from their dance cards, simultaneously, I suppose even you could arrange that."

She seemed really odd, more so than usual. Normally, she was sort of annoyingly, cloyingly perky, tonight she was solemn and . . . driven. As if she'd come hunting. A predator Miss Cassie is not. Yet, she'd stepped deep out of her comfortable, private country club zone, deep into "ethnic", "urban" territory looking for me, in this place, where it was painfully obvious she was unfamiliar with the terrain and terrified of the locals, yet had known *exactly* where to find me.

Someone was tickling her keys and getting her to play a tune she didn't know, or couldn't play correctly.

I almost felt for her.

"He'd said he'd sent you packing—."

"'*He* said . . . '? *Ren* told you that?"

"Oh, yes, that and lots more . . . whore. (Ouch.) The things you've made him do. Pulling him down to your level. No wonder that . . . that last time with me, he was so—. Why won't you leave him alone?"

I didn't answer that, angry people, especially ones feeling righteous, never shut up, so you might as well preserve your energy, until the opportunity when they wind down or worse.

"He . . . he actually cried, he came to me for solace and forgiveness and . . . ."

'Solace and forgiveness' . . . *and tears?*, from the hardass king himself? Pun intended. Someone must've gotten laid very "tender" and the like.

I didn't have to ask, I knew. Ren'd gone to her, wound her spring ever so well and gently, as she likes and craves, then sicced her on me. Goddamn that Guy. This was some of his shit, instructing Ren to use Cassie to fuck with me; and Ren, no doubt, having a fine time of playacting sweetness and gentility.

I am so not having this.

Fuck that innocent dupe crap, fuck them, and fuck her for being so fuckin' stupid not to know that silver spoon up her tight ass sphincter had evidently been stolen from someone truly innocent, by her hardworking, underhanded moms.

God! She's *still* talking, I wished she'd shut the fuck up!

I jumped down.

That scared her.

I was gonna hit her, but freaking her out seemed instinctively a more fun thing to do, which is what happened when I grabbed her by the back of the neck and kissed her, hard. Tongue and all. It wasn't great. Not because she's a woman but because she's Cassie.

She shrieked from the back of her throat, as well as she could manage, since my tongue was deep in her maw, as I also fondled her. It took her a while to think of it, and even longer to get up the nerve to do it; but, she finally shoved and I let her push me off her.

Interestingly, she didn't wipe her lips, or spit. Isn't that what most people do when something wrong gets in their mouths?

"Ren was so right about you, he said you weren't my friend."

"I always said I 'weren't' your friend."

"You want him for yourself. You're in love with him." I am not being nice to her anymore.

"I suck his cock, the way he likes it sucked . . . unlike with you, Cassie, who doesn't know what to do with one. Then, he fucks me, unrestrained, down my throat, in my cunt, and up my ass, until his cum shoots out my nostrils."

A visual exaggeration, but she got the picture.

"That's our 'love' making. We 'love' what we do with each other and to each other, and Guy watches us, then Ren watches me do Guy with whatever nasty little things Guy and I 'love' to do. Same bed, at the same time and sometimes, many times, most times, both are in me at the same time.

"There is no . . . 'love'. And, you, silly bitch, are the furthest thing from Ren's mind when I'm riding his brother's impressive cock, and his own long, thick dick is shoved, like he loves to shove it, to the hilt up my ass."

She punched me.

Well, at me, missed my face, and hit my shoulder. It wasn't a Ren punch, or as powerful as any number of other punches I've received from loving admirers while stalking that so thin and nearly invisible line between Crime and the Law; but, I wasn't feeling very Law-like, was tired of her not getting the point, and just really sick of stoppering, redirecting . . . the energy—.

I hit her.

She went down in a gush of blood, and I went down on her. Well, I jumped her ass to beat the shit out of her.

Someone . . . someone(s) were screaming my name, as if I were doing something outrageously wrong. Come on. A rich, former private school bitch like this needs to get a trouncing at least once in her—.

Che forcefully yanked me off her and flung me aside, as Rummel checked to see if Cassie were too damaged. I never noticed how badly off she might've been since, when I landed, I noticed instead, several yards away—Guy standing before a stooped down, near mirror image of Keanu Reeves, Ren. Both tall, handsome predators coldly surveilling the carnage. If dearest Che had charged a roof admission, he'd've cleaned up.

Guy tossed one of his fine, Irish linen handkerchiefs to me. —Oh. Red on my wet, hard knuckles.

Rummel called on her cell phone for an ambulance and asked Che to carry the bloody princess away, then she asked me to come with her. I turned to her to answer but . . . felt

Guy and his heat move closer behind me. I did manage to answer.

"No, Jilli."

"Artemis . . . Arie, come with me." She grabbed me.

"No!" I shoved her away. Hard. Which scared both of us.

"This isn't like you, Artemis." Take note, she glanced up at Guy with great hatred. "You're falling too far, Arie, and when this woman presses charges—."

Guy cleared his throat, he was laughing but almost attempting to hide it from Rummel, before speaking.

"She won't press charges."

"And, how may I ask, Lieutenant, *sir,* do you know that?" Jillian Thelma Rummel can be real imperiously snotty sometimes. I like that in her.

"Cassie's pride won't let her, and her mom won't either." He and Ren both snickered. I smiled a teensy bit. Jilli was not pleased with any of it.

"No, really, Detective Sergeant Rummel, there will be no charges pressed, I can assure you of that, and thank you for seeing to Cassie. God or the Devil only knows what got inside her and possessed her to come way down here in the first place. It's really good to know you're on the ball. However, we have private matters to discuss with Detective Belladonna, now. You're dismissed."

Insubordination or not, she plainly wasn't going to blindly let him give her orders.

"Artemis? Are you coming?" A loaded question that, and . . .

. . . I backed away, only stopping when I felt Guy's fingertips brush slightly down the bare skin of my back, then across my ass; an extremely sensitive part of me, as you well know. That was all. *I couldn't leave.* Jilli saw my face change and her voice changed in urgency to match.

"A-Arie?!"

"Detective Belladonna, come to me, please?" That's Ren.

I felt a rush of heat across my face, as I managed a glance at her, before turning my back to go to him, still kneeling a few yards back. I think she said she never wanted to see me again, then left; but, I'm not absolutely certain. Not with both Fellowes Brothers inside my head. Ren softly laughed.

"Our Cassie's not too bright, is she? And, I think, finally, she'll not want to ever see either of us anywhere near her again. Gosh darn."

He looked up at me and softly stroked my crotch, which ached terribly to have him, as I felt it cramp and wet its starving palate.

"Arte, I told you before how you should come to me."

I got down on my knees. No hesitation, no thought in the matter. Ren stood to his full six foot one height over me.

"Now, tell us. Who owns you?"

Since childhood, through job interviews, whenever I've been asked to describe myself, to say what is most important to me, as if I were dissolved like a chemistry project down to one element, the strongest answer has ALWAYS been one word—independent. My answer now was very . . . weak.

"No one—."

"Stop being a child, Arte!"

The pitch dark vehemence in Ren's frustrated, impatient voice should've, would've frightened anyone else; it made me remember his delicious impatience and force whenever he wants me, when he's inside me.

God. No wonder Jilli looked at me that way.

But, I didn't flush with hot shame this time when I thought of her. There can be a lot of power in . . . no shame and no pride.

Oh, yeah. Here's where I piss away my independence, as well.

"I'm yours." He was reaching for my face when Guy spoke . . . his tone a warning and his eyes relentlessly on me . . . .

"Ren?" Ren ran that same hand over his hair, instead.

"She said it, Guy."

"She didn't say the proper words."

"'Proper'?"

"It matter—."

"You and your . . . . I really want to fuck her, Guy! Now."

"Like Tsianina?"

After the mention of Ren's homicidally deceased wife, the rest was evidently a chastisement in a pidgin mix of Cantonese, Portuguese, and French, which is what they speak, when something's extremely critical. And private.

I gotta get into Berlitz®, Living Language®, or something.

Ren stepped aside, taking my power over him away from me and giving it to Guy, who waited, still as death, while his brother paced, barely contained.

"You . . . own . . . me." I knew before I said it, that it wouldn't please the number one guy in my life.

"Who owns you?"

Guy knew I knew he had me. That he was breaking me first. If for no other reason than he's far more patient than I am.

"René and Guy Fellowes own me."

The "Prince" nodded slightly.

Ren snatched me to my feet to stare at me as though to kiss me, but ripped away my bra's leather lacings freeing my breasts, which he hotly devoured. I held his overheated head to me, as I watched Guy watching us. Finally, Ren kissed my mouth, as he undid my pants, then stood back just enough to watch me wiggle them and my panties down my thighs. He stroked my bush, as he advanced on me, forcing me to the wall, as he unzipped and we both pulled his thick, rigid tool out.

He flipped me around, soft cheek to prickly brick, his one hand still laced through my pubes, and knowing I'd be ready and wet enough for him, as I bent to receive him, he pushed his cod to the hilt in me, forcing a throaty sigh out of me.

It was a peculiarly soft gesture for Ren, then he felt my vagina contract tightly around him and he moaned deeply. He loves to assfuck but when he's out of his mind for me, he prefers pussy. I used the coarse brick wall for leverage as he seized my hips and we pounded each other, as something caught my eye.

Che was walking up behind Guy . . . .

[story break]

I awoke again, alone, when the late alarm went off, and found a tiny choker on my finger; a large blue white diamond on a brushed gold and platinum band. Guy'd slipped it on while I slept. It was lovely. I was pissed, to say the least. It was always, *always* understood between us that we were together for the sex . . . not for . . . love. And, most certainly not marriage. Now, he gives me *this*?

A note he'd left said I shouldn't take it off, or there would be "hell to pay". *Seriously.* "Hell".

Well, to Lucifer's Daughter, Hell is home.

I left the expensive bauble back over at his place, where

he'd find it. He called later to ask to discuss it in person.

Remembering that I was dealing with Guy triggered alarms off inside me; but, I'm used to playing rough, and I'm used to knowing when to skedaddle. Normally. However, I hadn't yet realized I have absolutely no sense of decent parameters with either Fellowes brother. I bet you didn't think I even knew the word "decent", did you?

In what was getting to be a long stretch of uncharacteristic stupidity on my part, after my early shift *(yet still undercover at the strip club)*, I met him at Ren's apartment.

Mistake number . . . pick a number. I couldn't get out of Ren's, and I've gotten myself and others out of crackhouse riots in the middle of rival gangbanger wars. Guy'd sat there quietly on the sofa, his long arms spread wide across the back of it, with the ring perched on the tip of his pinky finger. Ren stood across the room, behind me.

I eloquently put my foot down. Explained that whatever had come before me, with Tsia, I couldn't do anything about it, and they knew it. No problem. However, I certainly wasn't getting married in any way, shape, or form. We were about sex, sensation. No love. No ring around the finger.

Note: Western Cultural Tradition. The engagement/wedding rings go on that particular finger, the Venus finger, because allegedly there is an important vein or nerve or such that runs from it and straight to her heart. So, to bind that finger meant you could bind a woman's wild, uncivilized nature and therefore forever join her to you. [Men aren't wild nor uncivilized, I guess.] Anyway, back to <u>this</u> ring.

I repeated to them that there would be "no ring", and absolutely no "cleave onto one another" marriage.

Running out of points, and tired of their annoying mutual silence, I headed for the door. Guy's voice was almost inaudible.

"Take her."

Ren struck a concussive blow between my shoulder blades, knocking me hard to the floor, before deftly disarming me of my Beretta. I fought—*kicking and scrambling*—even got a real good backhand on his cheek; but, outweighed and outreached by a superior martial fighter, I was soon disoriented from too many hits, and sacked over Ren's broad shoulder, as he schlepped me to his bedroom.

Guy just sat there.

My ears were ringing, as I heard him talking foreign on the phone, as I pulled it together, and made another attempt at freedom while lying on Ren's floor, after catching a second wind, which Ren promptly knocked out of me with a brutal, abbreviated shot to the ribs. He could've broken me but didn't. Then, he ripped off most of my clothes and restrained me with soft, buckled handcuffs at wrist and ankle on his bed, stomach down, my still trousered ass to the wind.

His bed, unlike his "playroom", didn't ordinarily come equipped with four cuffs, it was so nice that they'd planned ahead. Stupid me.

He cut off my fitted, stretch jeans with his trusty pocket switchblade. The fighting struggle between us was one thing, even the shredded clothing was . . . tolerable, being bound wasn't. I don't like wearing cuffs, snug watches, constricting collars, or tight, binding engagement and wedding rings. I don't like engagement or wedding rings. Period. Not on me.

"Ren, release me, right now!"

The fucker took his sweet damnable time about undressing where I could see him, as I struggled with the bindings. No wonder insane people get crazed wearing straitjackets.

"Let me go!"

He mounted the bed, picked me up by the middle to stuff

a pillow under my abdomen, then started with my left shoulder, with my Aegis tattoo. Some lousy sign of protection and guidance it was turning out to be. He kissed and licked, tasting every inch of me he could find, and he found *every* inch, before making himself at home over my ass, licking and kissing it, softly biting each cheek, then he parted them.

I was already breathing deeply, and completely wet; my cunt contracting on itself for want of him. I couldn't really see him clearly at that angle, as he blew softly on my most delicate places, then ignored them to kiss and lap at and around my bunghole, stiffly poking his harsh tongue, then heavily lubed fingers into its idle tightness. I held off vainly rewarning him about my detestation for being assfucked, before forgetting justified repulsion and nearly even the restricting bindings.

Ren brushed his iron cock through my slickness, hole to clit, over and over, before slipping something hard, vibrating, and about the size of an ob® tampon into my pussy. The damned thing felt like it had rotating ball bearings. What it did have was a remote control! Which he cranked up, letting the baby vibrator take its affect on me, as he squeezed thick, warm lubricant into my anus, prior to pushing his codhead into my slick, welcoming shithole. He patiently moved in and out of me, getting me used to the disconcerting, intrusive fullness of him, while his vicious, tiny collaborator quivered inside me.

The hard wall of his body flush against mine seemed to push the machine deeper within, getting an unguarded moan out of me, before abruptly banging my ass mercilessly, as with each maddening thrust the vibrator accented his every move. I prefer man to machine, but both? This was too much. I used the headboard for leverage, as I fucked just as hard back against him, before . . . .

Finally noticing Guy beside the bed watching us, watching me . . . .

[story break]

"Simply speaking, Arte, you're ours . . . mine specifically, in public. I'd put a hot brand on that beautiful, round brown ass of yours—." My gut churned at that. Guy doesn't "make up" scary tales to frighten his women. What he says, he means. Or at least is seriously considering.

"I can, you know, brand you, in many parts of the world; but, in lieu of that, this 'choker' will have to do. It's the acknowledged custom here, when a man wants to mark his woman as 'private property', 'off limits', 'absolutely do not touch', or fuck."

He stroked my body, possessively, proud in his ownership. *Their* ownership. And, by the way, he hissed in my ear from behind, as he mounted his favorite ride, that I 'don't want the punishment [they'd] deal' me, if I 'step out of line or take [his] ring off one more damned time' . . . .

[end of "Aegis" excerpts]

www.aegis.neale-sourna.com   **www.Neale-Sourna.com**

Novel excerpt from work in progress:

"All Along The Watchtower"
by Neale Sourna

From Book One

. . . He saw in her war tent, the roomy, collapsible sleeping platform, with its gold wildcat's pelt covering, but did not look at it overlong, assuming nothing except that she might simply thank him and dismiss him for escorting her through the two rival army camps, which from what he had seen of her personal battle skills on this first day of their pre treaty meeting, she had not needed aid. He remembered his best spies had said that these wild Steppe horsewarriors traveled with a degree of comfort befitting their wealth and strength, and they had said of her in particular that her skills were of speed, cunning, insight, and . . . magic.

anahk Tor did not believe in magic and one preternaturally prescient dream of this woman would not change that. He only believed in fertile brain, hot blood, hard bone, and sharp, tempered metal.

"My Lord General Tor, I would see your sword, if it is well with you. I believe its examination would pleasure us both, greatly."

He wore neither of his broadswords, and had not looked at her directly since entering her private quarters, and now did, finding her extremely close to him examining every aspect of his face, her apparent desire for him now, for the first time, boldly displayed.

Hers was a well-balanced, untamed face, with intelligent mid-dark eyes, which flashed quickly to the tune of her bright intellect, with richly dark brown hair of a deep red cast that in sunlight revealed it also had two auburn-copper streaks. But, in the interior light of the evening, her luxurious hair appeared soft black.

He looked again into her expressive, wide eyes, startling his heart . . . and he forced it to calm. For throughout the long day her hunger had been very much less obvious; leaving him in the dark without a guide in her shelterless, foreign land.

Tor did not move, as he flushed hotly throughout his body, whose temperature already ran naturally hotter than most men and was as torrid as the Egyptian summer fertile Blackland in which he and his brother had been born.

General anahk Tor, infamously known as "The Destroyer", did not move, because *this* woman already meant too much to him.

Dara's full lips bowed, half drawn, as if approving his restraint, as her fathomless eyes gazed on him, while she leaned into him and saw the stray brown strands among the deep black of his lengthy, abundant soft dreads and braids before sniffing the pleasant scent of it, her nose tip resting a long moment on the hard throb of his scaldingly warm throat, before her cool lips brushed . . . then rested on his, without physical pressure.

He did not remember telling himself to drop his well-held restraint; however, he must have, as he found himself holding her tightly to him and devouring his royal host's perfect mouth and tongue, as she eagerly devoured his in return.

Then, she abruptly thrust him from her. And, he reluctantly let her go, afraid she would tell him to leave.

He knew she saw the animal shiver that ran through

him at her touch, as she slowly took stock of him, becoming completely familiar with his angular, lean muscles under his long, dark green, quilted dress tunic, before undoing the gilded hooks of it and slipping it from him; clearly pleased with the sight of his strong, war scarred, bare torso and arms, while she took her time taking an appraising inventory of his dark and tanned skin . . . .

He was losing the vicious battle of that damnable shiver, as his flesh answered each time she touched him softly and sniffed him deeply and kissed and tasted him . . . delicately, voraciously, then delicately again, from head to waist, back and front, grazing her fingertips lightly up the backs of his leather-bound, iron hard thighs and across his even harder buttocks.

Very pleasant.

Even more than all that—well nearly more—Tor loved how genuinely fascinated and amazed she seemed by his hard-palmed hands, in her close examination of them; gently, then wickedly sucking the long, durable fingers which, at this moment, he felt to be inept and too brusquely rough for such soft, yielding fruit as *this,* beautiful mouth . . . kissing the cursed palms, that had been covered with hot blood and spilled viscera too many times to recall.

Dara put her nose again into the crook of his throat, sniffing, flicking and licking him from throat to nipple, where she paused to gnaw and madden him before resuming her tour to navel, stopping at the waist of his leather pants, teasingly pausing near the thickly hardening mass between his thighs, which she teasingly cupped . . . and lightly squeezed . . . making his desire to have more than her hand all too apparent.

Her smile now was full, not mockingly dismissive as earlier in the formal evening when she had found his gaze continually upon her, and had glanced down him at this same fierce bulge, now straining the leather that seemed just barely able to contain him.

She put his hand on her dress, over her breasts, before guiding his fingers to the many thin leather cords along both of her shoulders and arms, which bound her in the dress.

He smiled; her nipples were hard as wood. He smiled, recalling that earlier, when she had discovered him once again staring at her, and not glancing away, he had methodically looked down her and seen these same breasts tightly bridled under her full length, creamy white chamois dress, cut to fit snugly to display her womanly curves, as the thin, soft goatskin further softened by the warmth of her form, revealed the intimate shape of these very same nibs, as they had hardened before his delighted eyes.

She cleared her throat, to bring his attention back . . . to the many, many lacings in her clever garment strapping her in.

He truly enjoyed the time it gave him to detain the wild urge rioting within him while loosening each one; slowing revealing the remarkable sable brown skin beneath.

Then, having undone enough of them, she finally slipped the fabric down; exposing firm, round breasts with mahogany aureoles; an opulently full, athletic body. The whitened leather slipped past her shapely hips, he brushed his fingers against and through the dark, silken, curled hairs between her legs before tracing the faint, deep lance scar, etched into her left inner thigh.

Her patch beckoned him back and he knelt to kiss her there, to bury his nose and fill his head and lungs with her aroused, musky scent. He parted the hairs then inserted his long, strong tongue to lick the soft, plump, mulberry coloured, humid flesh within, as her fingers caught into his thick hair and held him snugly to her. Her outer body felt cool but was warming to his hot hands, for in contrast to the bold heat of

General anahk Tor, Princess Dara Jaxartes' temperature very often ran cool to cold.

Dara softly sighed, which encouraged Tor, as he stepped beyond his station and laid the War Chief and Royal Heir on her bed. He gazed and felt his way up her incredible body from toe to head, with his forcefully gentle tongue and lips, and paid much attention to kissing and licking the lance scar on her upper, inner thigh, where the flesh is always most sensitive, even for one so accustomed to the bare back of the horse.

When he continued his journey up and down her, the weight of his long black hair fell enticingly, purposefully across her, adding hundreds more "fingertips" to the many sensations he generated deep within her, making him pleased to see *her* now shiver as well, as he suckled her tongue, her lips, her ripe breasts, and her little cave of a navel, all of her soft, fragrant and tasty skin—then he paused in the same place she had stopped with him, his hand resting upon her. She was a little overwhelmed by him and that pleased him more, because he wished to please her and because it distracted her from touching him too much.

Her touch made him too urgent.

He was between her legs, stalling at her dimpled waist and looked up at her, teasingly, knowing by the feel of her, the sound of her, that she wanted more of him. He slipped his fingers into her and she boldly writhed against them, which pleased him, seeing that she neither hid her desire nor her pleasure from his eyes and ears, to leave him to guess, like so many others of her kind, of her status had before.

"Yes." She said in her Pers-Scythian tongue, one of the first words of that language he had learned and committed to memory this day. And, "Please." Which was in the Nilo-African High Court dialect of Her Father, which he understood better.

Tor spread Dara's swollen, fragrant cunt lips open, exposing to view the little bud of flesh that his father had taught him could not be ignored. He spread her wide open, until the tender, darker mulberry flesh gave way to the most tender and reddest of pinks, then his dark head dove to dine and drink of her freely flowing, sweetly salty juice.

He forced his hard, probing tongue deep into her, until, in sharp desire, she ground her delicious crotch into Tor's mouth, before again brusquely shoving him from her to watch, as he stood long enough to shed his now highly uncomfortable dress pants.

Once unbound by his leathers, she could fully see how beautiful he was and exactly how much he wanted her, as she slipped her thrilling, calloused, hot palm up his thigh, cupped his swollen balls, that burned her and took Tor's dark, hard cock in her eager hand. Dara bent her lips to kiss his shaft then lick and gently suck away his impatient precum at its head, before he kneeled and she guided him into her, causing them both to moan and sigh at full, deep contact.

[story break]

They were alone, it was eerily quiet, and she was standing in the water watching its placid surface. Tor was submerged, he had been for some time. Tor was . . . hotter than angry. He was incensed, and finally stood erect, cascades of water dripping from his long black dreads, his dark muscular back to her, and she waited till he whirled around and faced her; his eyes were not pleasant to view.

"Tor, do not be this way. You have duties just as I have; yet, I also have obligations to my bloodline and My Goddess."

"And what obligations do you have to your husband, Dara?"

"You are not my hus-Bänd. We are not wedded in the way of your west, Tor. I know what all that means, and as my officially Bänded mate you know I prefer you over all others; but, it is still necessary that I serve both Queen and Goddess, and the generations' long alliance we have with Rüsjmahadan's family. I will not be responsible for breaking ties with them because his parents should deem my lack of action on his moral behalf, in order to please you, as a gross injustice."

She softened her tactful plea.

"If I do not do this for him, as contractually obligated, it would be considered not only a personal snub, but one that would cut his family and people to the very bone and blood. It is not just tactical or political, it would be a *spiritual* error . . . a blood and spirit *curse* upon his new extension of their royal house. *I must do this."*

He was minutely swimming backwards from her, staring at her face, watching it, noting every expression on it and of every intonation of her voice, even the way she gestured to clarify her stance in this enduring public intrusion into their private lives.

"Tor, I understand and for myself welcome your incredible intensity, but you cannot allow what I must do . . . for duty, obsess and hurt you this way. Furthermore, my life, as I was born to it and chosen for it, will always be a public life, and, as my Bänd, so will yours."

"Dara, public is one thing; however, how is it you royals can always find some manner, *any* manner to share your beds? There will always be another and another . . . *duty*. Why . . . why can I not have one thing that is mine alone? I will no longer share my bed, my woman with any . . . ."

He did not bother to finish. His bed had never been so public before with this Mare Goddess' ancient rules and unrelenting hold on what was his.

Tor slowly submerged and stayed under until his lungs

could not bear it. In waiting for him, Dara moved back to sit on the low stone shelf just above the water, used for diving and lolling. The day, the sky, the air, the water, all were perfect as she intently watched like a sentinel for him. He slowly swam back to her as his lung's deeply refilled with fresh air.

"Woman, Princess, High Pries—. . . ." He corrected his linguistic error. " . . . Shaman Prime are there anymore *Ceremonies* I should know about?" She merely, sadly shook her head; this arguing and clarifying . . . his general opposition was draining the energy from her.

"I am again Blessed With Child by you, Tor."

She watched him closely, hoping this fact would ease the pain he continually felt. His chest swelled, for his heart leapt inside him, and he sighed deeply. He did not move or even seem to breathe for a long while, then slipped his hand between her thighs and touched the outwardly most female part of her. He touched her until she sighed repeatedly for want of him, then he stood and rather abruptly slid the most male part of him deep into her potent soft folds. He languidly moved within her, the both of them enjoying the intimately penetrating contact; then, brusquely he pulled all the way out of her.

"I understand about your duty, Dara, but I still do not wish it . . . here."

He pointed to his breast, pausing to see if her desire for him remained plainly visible to him. It did, and so he dove for the bottom of the river and stayed there past reason, past the limit of his lungs. He resurfaced close to her, his great dark passion for her even more rigid, as he barely shook the water from his hard warrior's body and immediately reentered her. She ensured his continuing presence when her strong legs secured around him. Tor loved being locked inside her equestrian legs, for as strong as he was, when she truly wanted to hold him to her like this, it was nearly impossible for him to free himself; physically, emotionally, or mentally; he did not want to be free.

He picked her up, without disengaging from her, and moved their lovemaking to where their things lay in the soft, matted, long grass. Tor knew it was Treason; but, nevertheless, he was weary, tired of wanting what his sacred mate could not give him, because of Her Goddess' constant, overly personal attention, and nearly exhausted of sharing his most intimate self with an entire nation and its too tangible Goddess, instead of just with this one particular woman.

[story break]

anahk Tor—*General to a foreign king, Lover to this one woman, Prince Consort to the Royal Heir*—bedded Dara gently, insistently emblazoning her with his dominant claim to her, with his mouth, his hands, and his cock; marking her with the scent of him, the feel of him, and with his virile mastery, as he rutted her need for him to the root and filled her longing to overflowing with his seed. The young colt may lie with her, to learn the proper ways of intimately pleasing a woman before his own marriage; but, even with Dara as teacher, the boy would never surpass Tor.

Dawn broke and she rose, taking the heated scents and comfort of her lush body away.

Again, Tor observed her vibrant nakedness, as she slipped on her seatless, leather riding leggings. He reached for her, slipping his knowledgeable fingers deep inside her from behind, as his other hand reached around to stroke her soft pubis and the wet slit between, luring her back to him. He licked, kissed, and nipped her buttocks and felt her vagina cramp and strongly suck on his fingers, before she stepped out of reach, with a half-moaned sigh. He knew that pleasing sound well. It said she was not angry with him for continuing to detain her, and that she greatly wanted him still. He lay back, as she slipped into a sleeveless tunic dress, boots, and jacket.

She finally sat beside him and gazed longingly down the full, strong length of him, filling her eyes, recommitting the familiar sight to famished memory. She stroked up from his bare foot, up the inside of his leg, feeling the hair, skin, scars, hard muscle and bone beneath.

She took gentle hold of his scrotum, before gripping his manhood and tenderly kissing its head, then took its full length within her warm mouth and throat a long moment. Releasing him, she kissed from the base of his penis, up his hard, flat stomach to dawdle with a lick and a long sucking nibble upon his nipple before pressing onto and reaching his mouth. She lingered there, her tongue dancing with his, until suddenly forsaking him, grabbing her pack, weapons, and riding bags, as she took full leave of him without another glance back.

[story break]

Tor rode off alone to the holy cave nestled at the bottom of an innocuous, deep hillock hidden in the trees. He dismounted several hundred feet away to walk the rest of the way, silently passing Dara's red war stallion and Rüsj's mount in the inside enclosure on his way to the inner, sacred sanctuary. He softly growled in the back of his throat when he heard the young Princeling . . . in heat . . . and heard "his wife". He knew her sounds well, her sounds while in sexual passion.

He hefted the sharp war axe, which had found its way into his ready palm for no other reason than it felt exceedingly good to hold this particular day.

Her silk gown was on the floor beside the boy's trousers. Her hair was loose from its ceremonial horsetail and the young royal's hands, lips, and tongue were upon her voluptuous, naked body. Dara was in desire's full flush; and when the Princeling lay back, Rüsj's young manhood, hard and fat as a

Nile temple column, was eagerly thrusting up inside her, possessing her, pleasuring her.

Dara never stopped her sensuous, bare ride upon young Rüsj's tender prick, as she opened her eyes, unsurprised to see Tor The Destroyer. She glanced indifferently at the axe, paying little heed to him or his apparent unspoken, anguished intention, except to acknowledge seeing him, before returning her affectionate full attentions back to her ardent student, as Tor's sombre, betraying thoughts twisted further inward, and he, with his axe and His Rage, surged forward . . . .

[end of "All Along The Watchtower: Book One" excerpt]

http://watchtower.neale-sourna.com
www.Neale-Sourna.com

Novel excerpts from:

. . . I bounded out of my seat and got another nasty, warm beer and drunk half or more, before she took it from me. She polished it off, gazing at me, making certain my eyes were on her, and her pink tongue, as she licked, then sucked the last foamy drops from the dark, hard bottleneck. I heard Hopkins laugh at me as, with a flash, he lit another cigarette.

"I'll make the decision easy for you, boy, get out while you still can. She tricked me into believing she'd be safer with me than in the asylum, and now she's expertly playing us against each other. I have the money, you have the . . . hard youth, and she has each of us, by our manhoods."

"There was truth in what she said. Somewhat. However, since, I'm her guardian, what better way for a 'delicate', insane young woman to control her older, male keeper than to suggest . . . I repeat, *she* suggested I lie with her." She stared round at him, in astonishment.

"Hoppy, that's not true."

She had lied some, but I wasn't sure when. And, now, she didn't seem to remember herself, exactly, where in their history they were, and I certainly didn't.

"Mommy's really mad . . . mad that . . . that I let you—."

"When I said 'no' to her, Day came to me, naked. You've

seen her considerable attributes and I may be . . . old and grey; but, I am a fully functioning man. She said she'd 'close her eyes' and I could 'do whatever I wished', 'pretend whatever I wanted', and 'use her however—'."

"*NO!* No. No. No. No. *NO!* That's . . . that's . . . !"

I was getting very much confused and was about to edge away. She uncannily, instinctively sensed it, shook her head "no" at me. I shook mine and shrugged. Abruptly, she was with me, kissing me, her whole body seductively against mine, her tongue in my mouth; usurping any independent volition right out of me.

I was so screwed.

Hopkins growled, deep in his throat.

"No!"

[story break]

Gist: Pizza Yutz was some Surgical Attending Physician from the hospital, where Hopkins had had her ankles cosmetically repaired. She'd called him before, well, paged him; Day doesn't like conversations on the phone. She'd paged Pizza Junior Surgeon once before, just to stretch her powers, to give herself a sense of power and independence . . . to feel another man's . . . hands on her, a man *she'd chosen*, "anyone" besides old Hoppy "groping and poking" at her.

I could tell through her words, that she was indifferent to our young medico; nevertheless, his very existence still annoyed me. Her reasoning was that, at a time like this, when she wanted to bust my nuts, keeping tabs on me, that she preferred "paying him for his eager assistance with a few lame fucks on the bike tarp, rather than get [Mrs. G] fired for helping". How considerate, warped, evil . . . .

She called me a long string of obscene epithets, the least of which was . . . "fucking bastard" before turning her back on me. That shouldn't have bothered me; but, it did. I walked around to address her face, she turned away again; we repeated the process, which pissed me off further. *I know.* She was yanking me. She was sincere about her feelings; but, she was still yanking me hard, because she could, because I allowed it, and we both knew that. I got on the bed with her. I shouldn't have. I shouldn't have touched her. Or seen the hot, salty tears on her cheeks. Or . . . kissed her . . . trembling, soft, yielding lips. Or . . . .

Somewhere in the night, I heard an overfed, slightly drunk Hopkins open her door, then curse when he saw me with her. She was happily cuddled and spooned hard against my back. He slammed the door.

* * * *

I'd just rounded the corner into the hall, mid morning, next day, having heard nothing, before Hopkins seethingly bellowed—.

"*You whore!*"

He backhanded Day across her high, rounded cheekbone. She moved with his action but still received a great deal of that percussive act, which caused her to hit the wall. I roughly grabbed his hand to stop him from striking her again. It was the first time he and I'd ever touched. The thought of striking him, like he'd struck her, occurred to me . . . but . . . there were no blows between us, because with about forty odd years difference, his smoking and no exercise versus my physical strength and outrage . . . I'd shatter him.

And, be promptly arrested.

Day for her part, remarkably, didn't shatter and break, despite his rough hand, as she'd apparently been prepared for it. She didn't stumble as much as I would have thought. Her eyes didn't water up. She didn't whimper. She didn't touch and soothe her brilliantly bruised face because this had obviously happened before, and explained how and from whom she'd learned to deliver a blow like that herself.

She straightened her dress and ignored both of us, as she limped away, using the wall's surface as a support guide while avoiding his contempt and my concern. She headed through the front rooms, then out onto the porch to sit, nervously tugging at her worn footgear, as she gazed far out at the water, as if starved to be out, far out beyond it.

"Hopkins! How could y—?! What is wrong with you?!"

I can't express the heat that radiated from the hatred and anger in him. If I had gone any further with my obvious rant, he plainly would've barred me from the house, from her. He might even have run away with her, in an attempt to do so, before I'd take her, because that sort of unspoken desperation, which so often hung about her now hung like ice floes around him.

His anger and fear were justified, because despite Day's behavior in the previous forty-eight hours, I'd've taken her from him at that very moment; but, legally that wouldn't have gotten us very far. I let it go for the present.

"I don't understand, Hopkins, wanting a woman, who so plainly doesn't want you. . . . Wanting her . . . forcing her . . . for how long?" I left out, "not since early childhood, I hope" and trailed him to the living room and its beachside, French doors, from where he assiduously observed every breath she took, while sitting on the topmost step.

"We came to a point, when she was yet a girl, but not a girl. She . . . would tempt me . . . in her calculated nonchalance, to make me want her . . . beyond all reason." That sounded familiar. "Then she'd callously refuse me, feigning indifference. But . . . ."

He discontinued abruptly, as if flash frozen, like a thought, a feeling, a memory freezes in the mind and chills the soul. There was a lie or something in what he'd said, I was nearly certain of that; but, I never could feel him, read him like I could her.

"She has the right to refuse you."

He smiled, if glacial blue ice can smile.

"Like I have the 'right' to toss an unwanted resident squatter from my house, who eats my food and fucks what is mine."

He had a certain valid point of perspective, though, technically, he had personally invited me to stay; but, I wasn't in the mood or mind to sympathize with a man, who'd been keeping the unwilling woman under discussion, for his own quite prurient self-interests.

"I'm not blind and she's not stupid. It's more than anticipating the fulfillment of having her want you; you entirely get off on controlling her, knowing she's dependent on you for every scrap of food, every piece of clothing, practically the molecules of air she breathes."

He stared at me a long while, weighing what I'd said.

"I do. I really do . . . 'get off', is it, on that, and no little slut deserves such treatment more than she. I rightfully, legally control the cunt and still she defies me, keeping . . . *herself* from me, hating the touch of the hand that feeds her, yet trying to play me for a fool, the ungrateful little bitch.

"Steve *[from next door]* saw her steal away the other night . . . after you. But you know that, don't you? You forgave her, didn't you? That's what I overheard her whisper to Mrs. Gorbachev. That she'd whored herself with two men to pursue you, eventhough she was in no position to really do anything to stop you, or to force you to come back. *And, you gave into her.*"

A shake of his head indicated a shift in his mood.

"I was ever so basically satisfied, before you arrived."

"She wasn't. Isn't."

"That doesn't concern me. What does . . . is that *sometimes* her body would forget its indifference and respond to me, not fully or willingly, but respond.

"You wouldn't understand the significance in that, because her response to you is so 'all-encompassing', I believe is the term she uses. She was like a barren, lifeless tree with a spot or two of greenery left to signify a lack of total death, but still worth keeping to gaze at and possess.

"Then you tripped over our horizon and she's suddenly full and ripe everyday, every night and I can see and feel and taste the edge of that difference, while she continues holding herself, her emotional attentions from me; and I resent her restraint *very* greatly."

He made a sound, a wounded deep growl.

"If I appear . . . if I am . . . greedy and harsh it is your fault, Mr. Gillespie. Her body now confuses parts of my touch for yours, warming that incredible body to mine. She detests that, even while she more obligates herself to me on your behalf. So, young man, this continuous stream of vicious discontent and acrimony you see, you have generated it. Which gives me heart."

I'm glad it gave him something because his little speech had eviscerated a gaping emptiness in me, as he swallowed like he was ingesting bile before staring through me.

"There is no secret in that I have always wanted Day and that I was, despite the tragic circumstances, glad to find an opportunity to make her indebted to me. And, I will be quite blunt and apparent. She will fulfill her proper sexual and emotional obligations to me and give me what I want of her or she'll never completely have what she wants.

"You, sir, came running down that beach to Day and gave me a screw to tighten right through the very heart and soul of her. I didn't have that before. In fact, I had nothing. Other than her nominal freedom, I had nothing with which I could get the better of her. Now, I know exactly what she wants. *Exactly, who she wants.* No. She'll never have it. Have you. Not completely. Not 'without strings'. Not ever. Not her. Nor you, either, Mr. Gillespie."

"You can't seriously . . . . I don't understand how—?"

"Please. *Please.* You understand it all just fine, my bright lad. And, you are a *very* bright lad, aren't you? Winning her to you, winning yourself free room and board . . . and especially bed? Look at us. Two grown men of the world, as our lovely, hothouse flower sits out there on her delectable buttocks and here we stand, her two industrious bees, flying busily around her, nearly always just about to fatally crash into each other over her.

"She's ignored me, said 'no' to me, and even grievously injured herself to keep herself from me; but, *now,* suddenly, she freely offers herself . . . to *me* . . . on the *gold platter* that is you.

"So, come now, we both know we need each other. Without me . . . she goes away. Without you . . . I can no longer control her. So it always is that the most valuable objects always come at a higher price . . . then that price, *if you're so very fortunate,* goes up while you own them."

He smiled in his malignancy at my obvious disgust for his calling her an "object" he *owned.*

"Bee to bee, Mr. Gillespie, I may be grizzled; however, I will have mine, even if you do register more trips between her soft, fragrant petals than I."

He stared harder at me, if that can be possible, trying to read me.

"Mr. Gillespie, just who the hell are you, besides a highly unwelcome guest?"

"If you want rent and board, fine. I'll pay it."

"Now, wouldn't that document me as a pimp." I didn't like his implying prostitution—.

"Keep your currency. When I have you tossed out on your ear, I want to be able to do it freely and clearly and spur of the moment. But, do tell me something. How thoroughly should I have you investigated? Give me a small hint of what they would find? What are you always running from out there, Mr. Gillespie? What is your personal world and business life, like that a vital, strapping young fellow, such as yourself, never has anywhere else to be, except here? What are your true intentions?"

"Investigate me all you like. Knowing more about me won't make you any happier, and they certainly won't find I was, for all intents and purposes, a former pedophile, who's keeping a woman prisoner, for my own sexual benefit."

He smiled sourly in thought.

"I suppose that is a fair description of me, Mr. Gillespie. But, let's not forget that you're benefiting, too. And, as long as I am benefiting, I have no desire to know more about you. Except perhaps, slightly wondering, excluding young Ms. Day, and since there's no ring on your finger, no talk of wife, husband, or significant other, that it would seem that maybe you too have been 'wanting' the unattainable and waiting for . . . something . . . someone. Who have you been waiting for . . . *Benn*?"

He said my name with distaste. It was the only time he didn't say "Mr. Gillespie", "young man", "lad", or "boy". It's psychologically notable that I glanced out at Day, who, in characteristic - synchronistic - out - of - earshot - eeriness, was staring at me with the bruise he'd put on her cheek plainly noticeable. Then, she glanced away and so did I.

I'd, again, forgotten the question, when confronted with

a query that could be construed as asking about my deepest feelings for her. Then, I realized Hopkins was laughing, loudly, at me; the laugh almost sounded empathetic . . . almost.

[story break]

My skin was crawling with too much energy running wild inside me and there was no one I could reasonably beat the shit out of, to make myself feel better. It was bad enough dealing with Hopkins alone but him with Stephie as well was too much. There's nothing like an enemy, who knows you inside out and isn't afraid to use that knowledge to cut you off at the knees. My only personal redemption was that we'd spent a lot of time apart these past few years and there was no way she knew my *every* thought, plus there was no way Stephie could know my *every* reaction when it came to Day.

I didn't know that myself.

Day touched my trousered leg, I pulled away then reached for her to rip the locket off over her head. I went back inside to get my keys and drove until I was afraid I'd run someone over in my preoccupation and rage. I found a patch of green and, inappropriately dressed, just ran until I'd run the circumference of it more times than I could remember and it was getting too dark to see.

Eventually, I drove back to the house where Day was sitting outside, her eyes hidden in the darkness by black shades, with her knees pulled up tight to her chest. All she had to do was tuck her head and she'd be the embodiment of the human football she seemed to be. Mrs. G was soothingly, absentmindedly stroking Day's hair, way past her usual knockoff time, which meant Hopkins wasn't around.

I asked if Stephie had called recently for him, she had. I'd spoken with Steph and she'd known when I'd get back. The bitch had warned him to not be around when she tilted my temper over the edge with her visual gift. At least she didn't want me going to jail for assault and battery or homicide. Also, Stephie, in her usual quest to control anyone and everyone, obviously hadn't imparted excessive info about me to fellow control freak Hopkins, or he would've been around breaking my balls about it, giving me grief in front of Day.

I told Mrs. G she could go, I wasn't going anywhere for the night and I'd "keep an eye on our little knifewielder". Mrs. G didn't like my joke or the fact that "Ms. Day" was "so extremely upset". I walked past them and inside, then heard Day softly beg her to "just go", that she'd "be fine alone" with me. Day's voice didn't sound rock steady on the matter. Thankfully, Mrs. Gorbachev left for home.

I like Mrs. G a lot and have a great deal of respect for her; but, she misses a lot of the crap that goes on, no matter how much Day tells her; plus, she's deferentially partial to Day's side of nearly everything, whether the girl is "extremely upset" or not.

I was reeking from my run and still "extremely upset" myself, because the past few hours hadn't actually abated my emotions much. I was pissed at Day for being Day, at my sister for being herself, at Hopkins . . . always . . . and was throwing a little self-loathing in for letting my libido and ego suck me so deep into all of this.

I also still greatly wanted to hold Day tightly to me, soothe and coo to her, and make it all better, take care of everything for her, which seemed a bit null and void after only less than two weeks gone. Despite that and more importantly, I'd been without her for all that time and, despite the video, I still wanted her very badly.

Being pissed is such a burdensome bitch.

I'd reemerged from . . . soaking my head in the tub. I would have stayed under longer but I haven't yet acquired Aquaman's® useful knack of breathing underwater. Or, of not wanting to be with Day. I was massaging myself . . . my masculine self, shall we say . . . geez, I had my dick in my hand, hazily thinking of her, when I turned to see she was at the door on her side of the bathroom.

"Come here, Day."

She looked at me oddly then disappeared, perhaps my emotions were too raw and naked on my face. I jumped out to pursue her.

"Day!"

When I entered her room she was half way across it, her back to me, frozen in place, evidently, since I'd last barked her name, knowing there was no way she could outrun me in this life or the next. I was sopping wet and leaving a water trail as I went to her and took a good look at the back of her; at her thick hair, the slope of her back, the round promise of her ass, which I covetously touched before spooning her against me. I know she felt my desire for her pressing hard along her spine, as I harshly whispered in her ear.

"Get on the bed."

She didn't move and I scooped her up and threw her on it. I made her face me and she modestly tugged her dress down, as I took my first really good look at her, since I'd returned and ended up watching homemade porn sent by my loving sister.

[story break]

He'd been back for weeks, and between Hopkins' regular His Royal Majestyness power trips and his added, extra, new illness-generated orneriness and her many divergent . . . moods eating away at mine, she'd managed to royally piss me off, again, in that pierce through me way only Day is able to do. Stephie busts my balls but Day, unintentionally or intentionally, can bust raw places in me no one else can touch.

And, despite my knowing why she was doing it, she still managed to get to me; only this time, I had no where to go, or run to, because I'd finally learned, slowly but clearly, that it was pointless to run.

I'd no where else I no longer wanted to pretend to go to, or pretend to run to, because I would come back to her. No matter that she was repeatedly convincing herself to anger me to make me go, because she still feared I would, especially now that she'd gotten a peek at how I used to live.

So, I sat my butt down on my favorite big armchair on the beachside porch, to stare out to sea . . . ocean . . . whatever. Considering her innate ability to get inside and read my most tenaciously secret mind and heart was as sharp as ever—her perpetual fear of abandonment by me wasn't completely groundless.

I was riled yet comfortably not going anywhere, as I half waved at Steve, our neighbor Penelope's husband. He habitually stretches in front of Hopkins' house, instead of his own. The stair to the beach floor is convenient to lean on and he likes to get a close peek at the lady of the house, when possible. No one but me was in sight, so, unfulfilled, he jogged up the shore towards my former hotel.

Hopkins was inside "doing his books". Actually, what he was mostly doing was staring at them and not triple checking and rebalancing his accountant's balances, as usual, because his numbing illness now thoroughly affected his ability to correctly understand that kind of blandly intense detail.

And . . . he was gloating, since Day had me thoroughly pissed at her.

The man was always hopeful in the idea that I'd get tired of her and go. And, probably just as hopeful that I'd never leave, since without me, he could no longer control her, especially now that he was too ill to manhandle her. So, though they disagreed on just about everything, my personal potential for abandoning her was the one concept Day and Hopkins mutually shared.

Poor Mrs. G had half mumbled that she was going to the store a half hour or more before, apparently off to buy pepper or such just to get a breather from us all.

Day wandered out, without saying anything to me, as she stood smack in front of me, blocking my line of sight of ocean, with her calico covered backside. I was trying to decide if I should let it go, move, lean to the side, or close my eyes—.

She turned around. Her skirt was up, her hand under its tail, her fingers wet from their warm activity between the "bearded lips of her womanhood", as my Peruvian, maternal grandmother might've said, once you translated.

I sighed.

The bitch was not going to fight fair or leave me be; she was going to drive me terribly insane by pushing me away then dragging me back by the delicate nads. I stared at her gently moving fingers, then glanced away after I realized I was "smelling her", "tasting her", "feeling the soft contours of those hidden folds of her" in my sense memory.

She recaptured my eyes' fascinated attention when she slightly fucked her pelvis against her fingers, with a grunting sigh, then came to me, letting the dress' hem drop. I pulled my head back a bit from her, but it wasn't much of a defensive tactic, and only halfhearted at best, as she wiped the taste of her cunt across my lips.

I pulled her hand away, which wafted her scent past my famished nostrils, as I barely managed a short wait before I licked up her flavor, which I believe she took as her cue. Day pulled a large pillow from the next chair to kneel on, between my thighs, which she ran her palms along the insides of, until finding the fleshy lump she sought, causing me to shift in my chair, but not to push her from me.

She kissed and licked and nipped at my bared stomach, unbuttoning my pants to hungrily explore me down to the pubic line, as, through my pants, she petted me, molded me . . . forced me far from my initial, aloof anger and to a lusting hardness.

"Pull out your cock for me."

My gut and balls yearned after the possibility she'd now aroused in my mind let alone the true physical ache her successful mouth and hand techniques were generating in me, as I glanced over the beach in harsh daylight, stretching wide and empty to either side of us. I glanced back through the window behind me and couldn't see anyone inside, only the reflection of myself and her and the world.

"Not out here, Day."

She smiled, wickedly. Wickedly, is the only way to describe how she smiled at me, as she pressed with delightful insistence on my perineum; on a guy, that's that real sweet spot between his nads and anus. She pleasurably pressed on it through the soft cotton fabric of my chinos, making my breath catch, especially as I had nothing on under the pants. In my remaining at the house with her, I'd taken to rarely wearing underpants when I wasn't going out. My buttocks, of their own accord, tightened, pushing me to be with her.

"Day."

I'm afraid it came out more as a faintly restrained plea than warning, especially after she unbuttoned her tightly bodiced dress, to the point of her breasts cascading out, which helped her petition to me a great deal.

"Don't say you don't want this . . . like this, Benn. That woman you were engaged to before, who wouldn't openly show her pleasure at being with you—not even privately—she never risked everything of herself for you, did she? And, you really wanted that, didn't you? You wanted her open to you, to entirely expose herself to you . . . shame herself even to the world . . . ."

She paused briefly.

"Yeah, especially that, because you wanted . . . needed for her to want *you* . . . *more* than anyone or . . . anything else, including her pride and her hardhearted self-importance." She winked playfully. "And, we both know *I* have no shame or . . . pride or . . . any of that. Right? *Especially when it comes to you.*"

I thought I heard a sound in the house but I must've been wrong. She was so deep inside my head, rattling around inside me where no one else but me had ever been, skillfully wrapping her will around the most protected, most delicate part of my ego. Day was being a touch playful but *she knew,* and she knew I knew, that she had me by more than my balls and enthusiastic cock.

And, I never answered her questions because I could barely think at all or manage to form an audible word.

That Steve would be heading back this way faintly occurred to me; but, my knees widened, giving her more access to me. She buried her face in my crotch and gently gnawed at me through the fabric, the enticing novelty of it, making me precum, as I pushed her head into me. She licked at the wet spot and huskily restated her previous request.

I complied and finished unbuttoning.

My pants were loose, with a wide opening, and it was little effort to pull my eager, thickly stiffening cock forth for her, the sensitive head of which she took immediately into her mouth, sucking off what was left of my "predew", which hadn't smeared inside my trousers.

Her mouth was hot and exactly what I wanted, her grip

on my shaft . . . firm and commanding. I barely cared that Steve was in sight and getting nearer, and would doubtlessly stop again at our stair for a last cooldown stretch and "lookey-loo" for Day. A "lookey-loo" being what Chuck's wife, who was in real estate, always called those, who looked but never bought.

Steve waved.

I didn't acknowledge his existence, as he paused for his cooldown, which never happened, once he saw Day's curl topped, dark head between my thighs, with a good substantial bit of my length rammed down her throat. He made some kind of noise, and she glanced around without letting go of me before pulling up and off me so he could see all, as she licked me, kissed me, reswallowed me, to the beneficial pleasure of both him and me—teasing him, pleasing me.

The thought *(another of those stray, stupid, inopportune thoughts of mine)* came unbidden—of how she'd come to her high skill level . . . which still bothered me. Not the skill itself; but. . . . Thanks a bunch for fucking up my head, Carlyle, your job is done.

Mrs. G was right about her though, Day is a nice girl, a woman a man can't help but like, most of the time. However, Doc - tor Car - lyle's descriptions *[I didn't tell you the half of his explicit details.]* of what he and the others had . . . *taught* her, flared and burned in my mind. It was the visualizing of Carlyle and . . . those faceless others with her, hurting her for their own entirely selfish pleasures; but, I let them fade with the warm manipulations of her tongue and lips and my own lust to be taken by her, in that . . . public and masterfully obeisant manner.

I know guys, who have a preference, a taste, shall we say, for sexual virgins and not often fucked "nonvirgins". These guys thrive on a woman's inexperience—if she doesn't already know what he can do to make her crotch ache, then he doesn't have to sweat it that she never gets hers while he gets his. I was never like that and I always liked that Day was experienced . . . accomplished even, which heightened the sexual high stakes game between us.

I just never liked *how* she had gotten her higher education.

Which probably is a half-hidden mental and emotional quandary for me, a little landmine filled quagmire that'll probably one day go BOOM.

Another reason, in case you hadn't noticed, of why I was still with her, was that Day was very right, more than right that I completely got off on her open, violent affections for me. On her open lust for me in general. On the fact that Steve couldn't take his eyes off what she was doing with me, as he crept up to the top step, while massaging himself through his jogging shorts, before half pushing them down to pull out his stiffened rod and balls . . . none of which fazed me. She was most likely a masturbatory sex fantasy of his already.

Even probably while he and Penelope went at it.

The fact that Day was messing with the minds of both of us simultaneously was something that should have horrified me, perhaps; but, I was the one who'd moved in, knowing she could only come to me after Hopkins, literally, came first.

She paused a moment, as if she'd heard or seen something then released the throttle control her hand had held on the base of my exposed shaft, so that I could pump up and fuck her throat deeply. Not something every woman volunteers for . . . or can manage, and with any other woman I'd try hard not to pump and fuck her throat; but, Day's nearly spoiled me with it. Swallowing a cock of any length or thickness is something I know I could never manage without tossing the full contents of my gut. The fact that she says she doesn't permit Hopkins to throat fuck her . . . makes it especially sweet.

On second thought, she has . . . *completely* spoiled me, perhaps even to the exclusion of anyone else.

While I recall long discussions in the dressing and locker rooms for years at work, where other men said they wanted oral or more oral, and also anal sex, as well, from their beloveds, and were not getting it, Ms. Day now had me entirely hooked.

Another thing you may not have perceived by now, because you fell asleep or have been jacking off, is that there's so much that goes on in a man's head, about rewards and punishment, lust and love, public and private. Evil and Good. Perhaps, I should've thanked Carlyle at that moment, as she attended to my . . . need, as I benefited from his astute and useful tutoring, which probably sounds like some sort of betrayal of her, by male bonding.

Well, someone once said, "Women want to be appreciated." Well, men want to be cherished and spoiled too, and worship of a man's cock, which is a major focal point of his own, by the woman he desires, goes a very long way.

Day had rethrottled my penis, curtailing my deep thrusting, because, in knowing my body, she knew I was about to cum, and she was in total control of this part of this fuck. She taunted me, instead of letting me cream her esophagus, by making me wait further, as she pulled off then rubbed her astonishing face against my hard cock, while she fingerfucked her cunt, which I could hear because of its extreme wetness, and which I very acutely wanted more than anything in any universe . . . .

"You fucking, controlling, little queen bitch. Mount me . . . fuck me."

The chair was big enough for us both, as I picked her up, not wanting to wait for her tender ankles to propel her up. She eagerly slipped onto my lap and I wasted no time entering her, the feeling of which pulled an enormous groan from me, and a sweet, throaty, little whine from her, as she put her hand on the large window behind us for leverage.

I only remembered Steve when he shifted his position on the step, which seemed to hold him transfixed, as if to say one more step up to standing *onto* the porch with us, was too close; but, where he was, was okay. I didn't fucking care. His new spot gave him a better view of her breast closest to him, as it jiggled voluptuously to our fucking rhythm. She whispered in my ear—making me party to her driving him over the edge, as I hiked the fabric up high off her ass, per her instructions, to let him clearly see her getting enthusiastically spiked on my dick.

She never again glanced at him, not even at his reflection. I know because her eyes stayed locked on mine, until she came.

I was glad she came quickly because I'd misplaced my usual composure and restraint . . . .

. . . and couldn't hold back, not once her strong vaginal muscles squeezed me and convulsed around me, and . . . *she sounded, like she sounded.* I came hard, blowing strong within her, and felt my hot, sweaty crotch drenched by her lust and my own. The humid air between us was filled with the thick scents of our individual arousals, which combined and thoroughly mixed into a deliciously heady perfume.

A dull, embarrassed, extended grunt came from Steve, as his strangling grip short-spurted and dribbled his wet splattering tribute to Day onto the floor; a little too damned close to my bare toes.

I was still inside her as I covered up her backside and breathed in her ear.

"You amazing, incredible cunt. No one's ever 'taken care'

of my needs like you. *No one.*" She liked that—her face is so easy to read about what she's feeling.

I kissed her a long while before finally rebuttoning her into her dress. Meanwhile, good ole Steve hadn't bothered to make eye contact or even say thank you, while putting "his business away" before running off, down the beach . . . not directly home, as usual. He went past it up the other way, out of sight. I don't recall ever seeing him face-to-face again or him ever stopping by to "stretch" or "cooldown" at the staircase while looking for Day.

I smelled cigarette smoke. The sun had shifted and when I looked back through the glass, Hopkins was just inside, breathing somewhat heavily. Must've been a great show. Better than the one he'd put on the first night. My cheeks flushed, not for what we'd just done, but for entertaining my smug, pain in the ass host. There was a wet spot on his pants' crotch where it was deeply wrinkled, as if he'd clutched it tightly for a long time. He stepped out, dragging the foot that no longer did all he wanted it to, and flicked his fag carcass to the beach floor. Litterbug.

He looked at me oddly—almost like he admired me. Not merely envied me but *admired* me.

Then he stared at Day, who, in his presence now crashed down off her hard rush for me, blushed horribly, in that strangely disconcerting manner of hers, of shifting from in charge adult to lost child in a second, as she turned completely away from him. Her movement said she wanted to get off my lap, but not to expose me to him.

Odd, huhn?

I put my dick back where it belonged and buttoned up my fly under the cover of her dress tail, before she dismounted, shook the tingle feeling from her lower limbs, then slipped past him back into the house without the tiniest glance at him.

He hungrily watched her retreating backside the entire time she was within his view, then he stared at me again, as if he had a question in mind, but didn't know how to ask it, yet seemed very certain I had the answer. He never said anything though or even grunted before he left; and almost right away, it occurred to me that she'd known he was there all along and had teased and entirely, thoroughly fucked . . . or mindfucked, as the case may be, the hell out of three grown men.

All at the same time.

I decided not to think about it too, too much and was still on the porch, facing the darkening eastern waters and sky, when Mrs. G got back. I kept it to myself that I loved the dried, slightly "starched" feel of my pants.

[story break]

They'd removed the locks completely at one time; but, Day'd become so unmanageable they'd been afraid they'd have to keep her sedated or return her to lockdown—neither option palatable to Hopkins, let alone Day or Mrs. G, so she'd gotten her locks back. I was told that Day never gave an explanation of what the locks truly meant to her. I found her sitting high on the bed with her back against the headboard, legs curled under her and hands frantically buttoning and unbuttoning several buttons on the front of her dress.

"What did he say to you, Day?"

She didn't acknowledge my presence in any manner, not until I reached to comfort her . . . . *She drew away, repulsed.*

[story break]

Eventually, as Mama would've said, "She took great umbrage," as she refused to be pleased by me in any manner, and, fell into a horridly frightening rage.

She hurried from me, in her determinedly labored way,

and into the kitchen, which has all new cabinets that she violently tested, but they held fast. She repaired to the dining room to the less sturdy antique sideboard, where she commenced rattling a drawer; the one that held the pointy forks and sharpest knives. Mrs. G keeps anything sharp or pointy under strong lock and key, of which I had a copy in my pocket.

It may sound stupid; but, Day's behavior was pissing me off; not directly but because she should . . . could do better than this, than let her emotions blow on every tiny breeze of her imagination . . . and at Hopkins' infernal . . . fucking meddling.

[story break]

I took my personal key and slipped behind her, where she was furiously yanking with all her weight on the drawer's handle. She stopped when she felt me behind and around her, and studiously watched, as I unlocked and slid open the drawer.

"I suppose you want one of those?"

Not until you think how much damage a knife can really do to a human body, do you consider, when opening a drawer for someone a bit knife crazy, just how many we keep lying around in our lives—for bread, butter, and steak; the Swiss Army, and the larger ones for cleaving and butchering. She chose well, a broad, sharp, step-down from a butcher knife, that was big enough with its nine inch blade to do serious damage to a man of good size and musculature, yet manageable for her smallish palm.

Day, when she's not in one of her many choppy, petulant moods, moves fluidly, with smooth, nearly languid motions, which, I suspect, is natural to her, being a dancer. I also suspect she knows she has a lot of time on her hands, so why hurry; besides hurrying pains her; but, she would have been a formidable professional dancer, if her feet had been anything like her hands are.

Her hands are terribly fast. Frighteningly fast.

Which is something you didn't need to know until now, because the really scary thing was just how lightning fast she took the blade, once she'd chosen it and then just as quickly moved away from me, to get a good . . . maneuverable distance, once she had it in hand. She'd grabbed it by the handle, flipping it under, to hide its length behind her forearm, which then languidly, nearly tranquilly, fell to her side and slightly behind her.

Having it in her palm seemed to give her some comfort, a sense of power even. I backed away from her; you don't turn your back on a pissed off, legally documented, insane woman with a knife in her hand. I wasn't certain if she were still completely enraged at me or not. Her temperamental fits with me never usually lasted long; but, this one was so abruptly brought on and more intense and laserlike that I was quickly reconsidering beating the shit and steak tartar out of Hopkins for whatever he'd taunted her with, while we'd been gone.

[story break]

Hopkins managed to crawl back to the steps and get himself up and mobile.

I deposited her in the tub, plugged it, and began filling it with cool water, very slowly warming it to heat her ocean cold stiffened limbs. She was in pain; but, she wouldn't cry out despite being curled up in its grip, then abruptly, completely submerged in her anger, her loss. She actually tried to inhale, right in front of me, and I dragged her back up to air, coughing and pissed to all high hell.

"Leave me be!"

"I'm not letting you drown right in front of me!"

"Then, look the hell away, Benn, cause I'm drowning everyday anyway. Let me go!"

I let her go, prepared to grab her again. Hopkins lumbered in and sat down heavily on the toilet's lid. She turned her back on us both, coughing and sputtering out water. She was very determined at this, if I hadn't woken from my deep sleep, simply because my body'd missed hers, she'd be dead. That's when I got a searing insight I didn't want.

"That's what you were doing on the beach, when we met."

She didn't look around or make a sound, only shrugged. Hopkins made some kind of strangled noise. I wasn't certain his sound was comment, fright, or a mere bodily malfunction. She was coming down from the rush and resignation came out on her like a cold sweat, as she trembled. I needed something to do, to reground me, since my brain was suddenly absent. I touched her leg.

"Don't touch me."

It was a serpentine hiss of a statement, and I ignored it, with prejudice, as I slipped my hand along her inner thigh through her wet dress.

"Benn, don't touch me, please."

She softly pleaded this time, trying not to look at me, as she shoved my hand away. She never shoves me away, especially when she's feeling badly. I'm pretty certain she wouldn't have argued, if I'd touched her again and I was about to when Hopkins cleared his smoker's throat, the sound of which stiffened her spine straight as an unstrung hunting bow and caused her to focus like a laser on him.

"Have I expressed to you lately how very much I *detest* you and hope you *die* very *painfully*, very *slowly*, very *soon*."

"When I die, you'll go back."

"I don't fucking care."

"Day?"

"Stop being nice to me, Bennet! I'm not your fucking project for your next seminar discussion." I wasn't happy with drawing her . . . ire, then she went back to him. "You've asked me why I don't . . . 'love' you, after 'all the things' you've done for me. Well, Hoppy, I do love you, as much as you love me. *Wait*, you don't love me, but you most certainly love possessing me, using me, requiring me to be . . . *nice* to you for my very little 'freedom'. Well, it is not worth it anymore."

"Day?"

"Shut up, Benn! I'll get to you, when I'm done speaking to my . . . guardian."

I was unthinkingly going to interrupt and she could see it on me. She has a razor mind and a laser tongue when she needs to cut someone.

"I know what you are, Bennet, I'm not stupid like he is. I have no old friends or dinner companions or portfolio monies to count or *anything* . . . to distract me from comparing what people do against what they say, or don't say. I know the truth and the lie when I hear them, even when they fit so nicely together on a tongue as articulate and sexually facile and useful as yours."

It wasn't very specific, her accusation, but I felt a deep coldness run through me, much like the shock of when I'd stepped into the Atlantic to retrieve her—it wasn't the water's cold I'd felt, then or now, but her coldness.

"Leave the lad alone, Day." She laughed, broadly, theatrically.

"'The lad'? When did the man you hate more than any other man I've ever known you to hate become 'the lad'? If he were the type to run away with me, you'd pull 'favours', spend all your estate to find us. You'd prosecute him to 'the fullest extent of the law'. Money and the law . . . and me, all made just to serve *you're* . . . *needs*. And, you'd separate us and hand me a blade and lick my ear with your suggestions, like a serpent, like you always do . . . murmuring . . . hissing hints of whatever you'd think would get the best effect, for you—that Benn's abandoned me . . . that I was going back . . . to *them*. Then, you'd step back and . . . ."

——for the COMPLETE Trade Paperback NOVEL . . .

Order HOBBLE through your *local* bookstore or

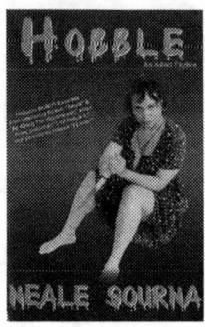 

ISBN 0-7414-1284-5   Trade Paperback
***or* call 1-877-BUY-BOOK [1-877-289-2665]**
www.InfinityPublishing.com

www.Amazon.com
www.BN.com **[Barnes & Noble]**
www.Borders.com
www.Waldenbooks.com
www.Fictionwise.com
www.Powells.com

and at other online sellers
and your LOCAL booksellers

**ebook editions *[Adobe, MS Reader, Palm]*
available through Amazon, Ingrams, & more**

Adult Fiction *[Explicit]*   *www.PIE-Percept.com*   *www.Neale-Sourna.com*
Buy — *HOBBLE* — Now at 1-877-BUY-BOOK, and online internationally

Also, visit us at www.CafePress.com/NealeSourna

Women's Clothing

Men's Clothing

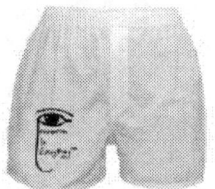

Posters & Prints

Cards & Journals

& More

Adult Fiction *[Explicit]*   *www.PIE-Percept.com*   *www.Neale-Sourna.com*
Buy — *HOBBLE* — Now at 1-877-BUY-BOOK, and online internationally

www.ingramcontent.com/pod-product-compliance
Lightning Source LLC
LaVergne TN
LVHW021943060526
838200LV00042B/1910